A Mage in Summer

A Mage in Summer
Olivier Cadiot.
Translated by Anna Fitzgerald.

Copyright © 2020 by Olivier Cadiot, Anna Fitzgerald, and Diálogos Books.
Initially published by Editions P.O.L, Paris, France, 2010.

Book design: Bill Lavender
Front cover photo "Sharon in the River" © Nan Goldin, used by permission.

This work received the French Voices Award for excellence in publication
and translation. French Voices is a program created and funded by the French
Embassy in the United States and FACE Foundation (French American Cultural
Exchange). French Voices Logo designed by Serge Bloch.

Printed in the U.S.A.
First Printing
10 9 8 7 6 5 4 3 2 1   20 21 22 23 24 25

Library of Congress Control Number: 2019948299
Cadiot, Olivier
with Anna Fitzgerald (translator)
and Cole Swensen (introduction)
A Mage in Summer / Olivier Cadiot;
p. cm.
ISBN: 978-1-944884-44-4 (pbk.)

DIÁLOGOS BOOKS
DIALOGOSBOOKS.COM

Also by Olivier Cadiot

L'art poétic', P.O.L, Paris, 1988 - English translation Art Poetic' by
Cole Swensen, Green Integer Books, Los Angeles, 1999

Rouge, Vert & Noir, BLOCK Editions, Paris, 1989 - English
translation *Red, Green & Black* by Charles Bernstein, Potes &
Poets Press, USA, 1990

Roméo & Juliette, P.O.L, Paris, 1989 (text of Pascal Dusapin's first
opera)

Futur, ancien, fugitif, P.O.L, Paris, 1993 - English translation *Future,
Former, Fugitive* by Cole Swensen, Roof Books, New York, 2004

Le Colonel Des Zouaves, P.O.L, Paris, 1997 (theatrical adaptation
by Ludovic Lagarde, 1998) - English translation *Colonel Zoo* by
Cole Swensen, Green Integer Books, Los Angeles, 2006

Retour définitif et durable de l'être aimé, P.O.L, Paris, 2002 (theatrical
adaptation by Ludovic Lagarde, 2002)

Fairy queen, P.O.L, Paris, 2002 (theatrical adaptation by Ludovic
Lagarde, 2004)

14.01.02, P.O.L, Paris, 2002 (recording of a public reading of Retour
définitif et durable de l'être aimé at La Colline national theater)

Un nid pour quoi faire, P.O.L, Paris, 2007

Un mage en été, P.O.L, Paris, 2010

Providence, P.O.L, Paris, 2014

Histoire de la littérature récente – Tome I, P.O.L, Paris, 2016

Histoire de la littérature récente – Tome II, P.O.L, Paris, 2017

Translations

To be sung, Gertrude Stein, Éditions Actes Sud, Arles, 1995

In *La Bible* (new translation, Bayard, Paris, 2001), *Psalms* (with Marc
Sevin), *Song of Songs* (with Michel Berder), *Hosea* (with Marc
Girard)

Katarakt, Rainald Goetz, 2003 (unpublished)

Oui dit le très jeune homme, Gertrude Stein, 2004 (unpublished),
Staging by Ludovic Lagarde, Avignon Theater Festival, 2004

Introduction by Cole Swensen

The truly uncanny aspect of Olivier Cadiot's work is that it's all true. Strange accuracies fly out of seeming absurdities, lighting them up from within. It's a new take on realism that's as optimistic as the 19th century version was pessimistic. Of course, the definition of realism is endlessly debatable—and endlessly debated—and while Cadiot himself would, no doubt, never have used the term, his work, fueled by a raging exuberance, keeps bringing us up, face-first, against visceral moments of pure presence—than which no realer thing could or can be found.

And then there's the woman who opens the book; she's real; her name is Sharon, and she is standing in a river, and the well-known photographer Nan Goldin is there too, standing just outside the frame, but because it's the frontal frame that she's exceeding, she's suddenly occupying us—and /or we've just displaced her. It's a jolt—and one that locates us even more firmly in the real that this work constantly unpeels.

Meanwhile, Sharon is still in her river, occupying it in order to in/con/re or simply fuse it, in order to create a liminal space, a space that is 100% liminality; therein the body can only dissolve, managing the metaphoric and the metonymic with a simultaneity that allows each to open the other on up. Charging the water: Sharon arcing—rather electrically—between a concrete visibility and a nether, and further, region of open interpretation—where the mage can take hold. This, in a reductive and wayward sense, is the essence of the book.

And we're still at the first paragraph.

Cadiot has, as has his family for generations, spent large parts of the year at a residence along a river, the Dronne, in a small town 103 km northeast up the A89 from Bordeaux, and while this is not the river that Sharon's standing in, it is the river that blends with hers to create an ambient flow that gains momentum throughout the book, gathering into it and sweeping along with it a profusion of particulars, all of them real. Or true. One of the things this book asks of us is to make that distinction.

For instance, historical traces can be found of many of the characters who flit through the text: In addition to Sharon, Éliphas Levi really existed, as did his wife, Marie-Noemi Cadiot, and all the other people in their cameo appearances, many of them the writer's ancestors.

But we're still wondering—who's the mage?

Éliphas? Noemi? Sharon? And what's the relationship to magic? Robinson? The only thing that most of us know about magi is that they come in threes—and that they haunt around in the background like a Greek chorus or chorus line—always seeing, playing the witness; the world requires a witness in order to come true. The mage is the witness, is the Angel of History, is one of those things, one of those three, bearing gifts—Benjamin, Klee, and an amazing accumulation of everything we can't quite see blocking the way.

The book is also true to Cadiot's own life; it's the only book he's written that is, effectively, autobiographical. It boils down into a disquisition on his life at various levels and in various directions:

1. There's the initial level of the historical-biographical

elements: The mage as family member, the mage as precursor—Éliphas Levi, author of Histoire de la magie and La clef des grands mystères, a radical socialist famous in the mid-19th century for reviving occultism in France. He became a strong influence on the Order of the Golden Dawn, on Aleister Crowley, and, later, on Helena Blavatsky. And his wife was Olivier Cadiot's great-aunt Marie-Noémi Cadiot; she eloped with him at the age of 17, escaping from her exclusive boarding school in Choisy-le-Roi, and became a noted sculptor, poet, and outspoken feminist, fusing socialism and feminism in the service of the 1848 revolution. Googling these people is well worth the time—look for M-N Cadiot under "Claude Vignon," the pseudonym she adopted, as did so many female writers at that time, to gain access to the conversation—literary, and above all, social and political, and above all, poetic, infusing descendants with infectious questions about the role of language in the art of magic, and vice-versa.

2. Robinson, who appears, slipping quietly in and out, and finally, just out, is perhaps the most autobiographical gesture in the book; the character of Robinson Crusoe has filtered through Cadiot's texts for years. The easy thing to say is "as an alter-ego," a form of identification through displacement—and that's clearly applicable—the individual, as a product of family history, cast as outcast— one of the principal M.O.s of the nuclear family with the messy collision of imperative conformity and insistent individuality at its core. But Robinson is also the mechanism that lets Cadiot slip past that basic isolation into a more intricate and enabling one. Robinson Crusoe, fully adult and solely responsible for his own fate, is the magician who can

construct an entire life out of absolutely nothing—his magic finds him an island, and then and thus, finds him on that island, re-writing John Donne: I'm sorry, old friend—what a good idea you had, but it just didn't work out like that—Cadiot has described Robinson as a frontier that moves. Islands become archipelagos; isolation becomes invention, to the point that you invent the footprint of another in the sand.

abracadabra-i-am-not-that-man-alone abraca-there's-now-dabra-a-world-that-me-surrounds abraca-only-the-lonely-is real

3. And that really is his father dying in section 2, and his mother throughout section 3, and he really did sing her last words at IRCAM. And visit bosons at CERN.

And yet it's a story with a happy ending—it comes full circle, back to the river, back to a grand dispersion in which it all, finally, comes together.

A Mage
in Summer

Olivier Cadiot

Translated by

Anna Fitzgerald

DIÁLOGOS BOOKS
NEW ORLEANS
DIALOGOSBOOKS.COM

1

Saw a photo in the paper today, a color photo, woman in the water, a river, a man? She looks relaxed, holding still like that, arms crossed, her breasts pressed against her chest, her wet hair in short blond coils. What's striking is how calm she seems, just someone in the middle of a green river, a fixed point in the current, seems to be thinking of nothing, just breathing. Now inhale, and exhale, waist-high water, body turned into a barrier, just like that. It's something to see, two wrinkles of water accelerating around her hips, she's half-bathed in coolness, half-bathed in sun, perfect. The water is green, I checked the color value in another river, it's approximative. The camera selects the green by itself, the good enough green, and the image captures what anyone would feel, planted like that in the middle of the water, a wave of the wand, click-click, and I'm gone. She wraps up all alone in her arms and instantly, all thought disappears, a sudden idea, ah! I'm a statue now, just like that, a barrier that everything turns around, filaments of water, chains of cold molecules forming whips, like the lassoing aquatic grasses that colonize rivers in slow, undulatory sway, silvery water robe and dragonfly green lamé. She takes her place, in heaven, equilibrium on the dot.

I wish I was her.

She seems content there, feet firmly planted on the bed of flat stones, so content she forgets her body, no need to present herself, nothing to declare, she's finally someone, unisex, in her prime, her hips soft and white, her shoulders tanned, except for a few pink peels, like a farmer, a woman turns ends up into a man, or vice versa. She isn't swimming, she's soaking, immersed, restoring. At work on her well-being. A carpenter removes the sweat and sawdust from his torso, a hunter undresses in the cold water, a conquistador stops to eat his lunch, Saint Sebastian at peace before the arrows. Go ahead, close your eyes, it crackles all around! Plop, Milky Way, magnesium, a green cutout is imprinted in the dark, a burning outline in the shadows, a little character crosses the river, while the shape keeps telling us: Of course it's her, why yes it's him, the minimum threshold below which you can't recognize anyone. X in the river.

I should draw a picture.

A sketch as simple as music heard at a distance, across a courtyard, through a window, can't make out the instruments anymore, only a voice that insists: I rise, I fall, I return, I start, I loop back, I disappear, I augment, I repeat.

You say, but is it good to be reduced to an automaton? Of course it's good, of course it's good, but why? Why is that everyone's dream? It's always been the dream: an automaton that cries out, why? How is that the dream?

14

She looks like a mare.

Like a gelding with her tousled mop, a horse made of wood, a statue made of flesh. Always something else. It's funny, she's so simple and yet she makes things so complicated, she catches my eye, multiplies, sends me signs, opens up infinity by the bye. Already seen, somewhere for sure, in a corner of memory. And again, in the campsite scene of a Western, using her saddle as a pillow. Dented red percolator, freckles and requisite sponge bath on the edge of the prairie, suspender snap, mirror hung on a tree, the stock Irish-Viennese moment, the river enormous and the shirts blindingly white. People jump from a pontoon in slow motion.

Claquette.

She blocks the way and water passes around her, running by her, magnificent. It's summer and marvelous. I love summer. Let's relax for a moment like she's doing. Oh I can imitate anyone I please, easy as a song. And she's imprinted on me, so I slow down and relax. Soft waves glint all around. God, I'm good! I like reconstructing the water's flow, it's motionless and quick.

I should draw a picture.

A point, a cross, an X in the river, and ffff-llll on either side, wavy lines to show the current that skirts around her.

And another X to show where I am, like that author who, in recounting his childhood, drew a picture of his bedroom and wrote Me in a corner.

You could say I tend to drift.

By projecting myself so much, I diffract. I'm in the aquatic grasses.

As if my ashes had been spread over a landscape, here, there, everywhere, I'm in the grass.

Let's draw a watermill.

Hmmm, fluid dynamics. Look, the water turns and, before flowing into the black hole of the blades, seems to stand still. You can see through it, like a block of ice that isn't cold, it's thick, like oil, slowing everything down, a transparent block, a magnifying glass, hmmm, you can see through to the bottom. Golden sand at the bottom. Sneak up on things from behind to surprise them. If an image is a building, use the side door for once. With illuminations like that, I've become a visionary. I'm disciplined, follow instructions to a T and have racked up experience.

Flight time.

I train.

All sweat and willpower. It's simple, I replay certain scenes over and over, like repeating a movement endlessly. Then I take to the air, streamlined. You can add beings and things in whatever shape you want, just like that.

I have an eye that goes underwater for diving, an eye at the right distance, like the lenses you use to watch animals, from just the right distance. You don't see them watching you, you don't meet their gaze. You see yourself in the empty sphere of their eyes.

You're alone with them. That's what I like about X. We could be alone together. I can feel her marbled body, its weight and exact softness. I want to see her green skin underwater. I want her skin, I want *under* her skin. I want to live together quietly, swim together gently. Escort her for a spell underwater, where it's cool and dark. I'm a fish in camouflage, gliding beneath the grasses so I can edge in unnoticed, underwater subterranean. In the deep, in the water, in the deep of the river. I can sing with my mouth closed.

A diving singer.

It's possible.

I'm plastic, I know how, I have experience. I'm alive and in constant flux, I wrinkle and fold. For my color, I choose old rose No. 57. Not fleshy enough. All right, I have an entire catalogue, I marble myself slightly, choosing a poorly photocopied Titian. I roll myself in a tapestry, as in a crinkly sheet for showing an outdoor movie, I drape myself in river, or in a water lily painting, stream sized, a tapestry the color of wading. I'm tone-on-tone.

Pike-fin shading.

The colors bleed. By chance, the newspaper image is a poor reproduction. So much the better, it speaks the truth without realizing it. Pravda. The colors have shifted as only nature can shift them. Fluorescent green water and electric grass.

Extras pop into this augmented nature.

It draws you in.

The screen used for printing is overly realistic, adding mosquitoes and sun sparkle everywhere. You can almost see the air vibrating, the clouds of additional atoms, or our very approximative idea of them. It's the beginning of the 21st century and we're representing atoms as little cosmologies with multicolor balls whirring around planets orbiting at top speed. But we already know how much emptiness there is everywhere, and we'll soon learn that matter takes the shape of whips, lassos and filaments.

Just like that.

New ideas using old images, but it works. That's how I envision quarks, even gluons! Vibrating, turning, bursting in air like fireworks. It's amazing to see someone's atoms.

I'm a mage.

What luck!

I close my eyes to see, since you don't see the same way with your eyes closed.

Who said that?

For my next movie, I'm going to close my eyes.

Closed camera.

Interior crystal ball.

Take 1.

I can mix my favorite images with everyone's, it's marvelous. And in any which way, that's an artist for you. It's the explanation that's dangerous. But relax, we're not here to write a three-part thesis.

Vacation time.

Nothing to declare.

And then, people are used to image-trafficking. A simple ad for the utility company is more improbable than *Nadja*. What's modern has been seen a thousand times. Everybody knows it, and knows it everywhere, with the little interludes that refresh the brain, the magical slates you see everywhere, on screens, in hospital waiting rooms, with the book-computers and new tablets made of electric wax. The abstract, the dreamlike and the superimposed are everywhere, monochromes in the recovery room, plastic sculptures along tram lines. All of it as pleasing as the pictures of poppies that used to hang in kitchens. It's a way of dressing up the things you want to sell on the mass market. And now everyone's used to it, it's as accessible as the Lascaux caves.

What a marvelous heritage. And if modernity solves half the problem, as one great poet said, that's pretty good, there's no one left to convince. And no one to keep us from saying what we want. Don't ask us to be logical when your kids can paint like Picasso before they're five.

Vacation time.

Who said they'd make their next movie with their eyes closed? What a good idea. We're off!

Movies are good.

People look day and night for what you've loved, stake out a location that's more or less a match. It's practical, they take you to an unknown place X where you say to yourself, Wow, this is exactly like my place! That's my dog! That's the same guy I knew. Hey... that's my mother. Almost the same, it's even better when it's almost the same because it's not your mother at all, how relaxing! Make us a composite sketch of the beloved. Something approximative. Oh... your mother has one green eye and one blue?

Sorry.

But overall, it's okay. Let's go! Flexibility. Adaptability. Modernity. Efficiency. You can do whatever you want, film angles, dive under the skin, go anywhere. You can even have eyes in the back of your head, and step outside the body to see yourself from above. Like that, very practical. The landscape is bigger than you could imagine, I didn't realize there was so much green here! It looks like an abandoned landscape. An enormous hodge-podge of plant life. Set up, film, look around. A river's edge. A real labyrinth.

I look at it from all sides.

Things get clearer as I go forward.

As in life.

Descent on the water between the irises. Articulated, pneumatic camera on springs, servocontrol. We move along the landscape, filming gently, it's quick and relatively slow, in the way an airplane seen from the ground looks like a snail track on a blue scrim. Above all it's stable, an absolutely stable and regular flow. We walk with our voices on this rail, using soft *Magnificent Ambersons* tones, imagining people successively lodged in the landscape. We tell each one's tale, the little dealings, the little memories, voices bursting out, each one's legends, little worlds side by side, a descent through the family tree branch by branch.

We film slowly, 360°. Centuries seem to pass, time really has time to change. Then touchdown at last, we're free, no ties. In one sequence I zoom in at a gallop, moving from the cosmos to the earth in a single dive. I enter the leaves. Have you ever fallen from the tip of a sequoia *giganteum*?

It's quick.

Where we land, the oblique slant of light turns the little patch of wall a bright yellow. Yellower, oranger and very quickly redder than is natural, if nature amounts to life seen in the paleness of ordinary time. Oh, the leaves are so red, it's autumn already, and cold. Pretty soon it's winter.

Let's go inside.

We move through the leaves. Like a missile finds its target by detecting heat, crash, angel landing, flash, through panes of glass.

Anyone there?

Home sweet home.

I go in with my eyes. Like that. Hmmmm, the hero's neurons. It's the first time I've seen my insides in color.

Round room.

We're comfortably seated, hospital-house, studio, white room, machines everywhere. All of this in a cabin slung from tree branches. A tower camouflaged by the weather. With loopholes for keeping watch over the countryside. Timeless Gallo-Roman. I mean strong and solid. Modern in old clothing.

Keep your hat pulled low.

Oh.

The brilliant idea of installing an office in the kitchen, or vice versa. A guy can roast a chicken while cobbling together a life. I have combo machines, ideal for a Me. Brain-controlled, always on, like these stoves that never turn off. Stick the pie in the right slot. No more thermostat.

You won't grieve for anything.

That's what the user manual promises.

A machine with the best advantages of all the discoveries that went before it. No technical nostalgia: an object made of wood and copper with latex parts that perfectly imitate the skin's elasticity and even its heat, but the reinforcements are titanium, the manual whispers. Mouse buttons and voice control, a billion pixels, little indicator lights burning blue. And we have a memory for everything: depth of the negative, contours of the stereoscopy, enormous vibration of the black and white, sepia and charcoal of the erstwhile dead.

And the oil effect of the autochrome process?

Absolutely, the manual is quick to add, you'll get 100% deep color, fruit vibrating with light, orange peaches on a Chinese blue plate.

Agfa? Fuji?

Of course!

How about sharpness?

Everything's cutting edge, superdigital. No losses. We've got everything. No nostalgia. Progress without losing anything. Colors crushed in a mortar. The smell of the projector, dust in the beams, the smell of the glass-bead screen + augmented reality. We keep everything, the lost effect as well.

We can even make repairs, declares the all-knowing manual.

Look.

It's like a plaster cast, it mends. Or maybe like shredded linen? Something cauterizes the scenes. Flaking material, washed-out colors, scratches, burnt negatives, fragments of missing people. Put the dead and the living back together at the right speed, the manual whispers.

Rabbit!

Sudden order via brain controls, and a rabbit steals into the kitchen, a good little virtual rabbit that's so precise, you can see its heart beating under its fur. Just before the sacrifice on stainless steel. You want an anamorphic skull in the air. Holbein kitchen function. That's it! I think action, then motor, then your father takes a seat in the chair opposite you.

A sort of father.

Like an old man lost in the street.

Like an image of him, it's approximative.

It doesn't matter.

Why my random-access memory is so good.

It's new.

Find whoever you want.

The manual promises that, too.

Launch a search.

Every image contains another.

Ad infinitum.

You just have to pick one.

I try this with that, in back, my heart laid bare, and fffft goes the soft tape, the magnetic tape in its metal box, and in comparing, embedding, superimposing, you realize sensations are things.

You can touch them.

They take up space.

They bristle and edge.

Solid songs.

Am I the loveliest one? worries the manual.

Ah.

You can spin them through the air, from the other side, backwards.

Everything's sharp.

Infinite sharpness, the same crispness in the folds, everything's creased and crisp, the narrator kisses his sweetheart, sees her tooth enamel 100 yards away, counts every strand of her hair, admires her beauty spot, the ad hoc moment, the pores of her skin are blinding us, oh a kiss was never quite like this, the slightest quiver of her upper lip activates thousands of little sensors around the lip opposite, yum.

Technical stuff is fun.

You tell me the first woman I kissed was a life-sized marble goddess holding a candelabra, lighting a stairwell. Lips of stone and a vertical vortex.

I was pint-sized.

In a corner of this entryway, on the black and white marble tiles, a bench, a trunk covered in studded leather, big enough to be a coffin, big enough to disappear into.

Stop.

I don't need this machine.

I know how.

I do everything with my eyes closed.

And it's live.

Just like that.

I really am a mage.

Back to our bather.

Still there, in the flow of the current. She seems content. Half warm, half cool and still motionless. She herself is someone, is herself someone, is someone herself. Someone of herself. X is tenacious, *headstrong*, like they used to say. She's realized she has a body and holds to it.

Some days it's better to stay calmly half-submerged in a river, without a thought in your head. Whhhew. Relax, don't even take yourself for what you could be. Merely become who you are and voilà! You fold into the void of you.

The living void.

Life is good.

Self-center, lights out.

I'm flesh in the middle of the water.

The bugs bug me.

Relax.

I can't remember who said in essence: I've endeavored all my life to be an ordinary man. Well, our X, he or she has succeeded.

And there's no use telling the world, just do it.

Chapeau.

Follow her lead. Being a mage, it's practical, hop right out of your self, watch, just like talking, it leaves, cries out, heads into the void, death, fireworks.

Just like that.

I can draw with my body.

In a snap, I dive into the crypt, green and gold. Into a hanging bubble of green.

I'm here.

The cross, that's me.

The pebbles gleam and the current glides, a net of glass spread over the sand, tchick, sparks.

I wonder what the Native Americans call mirrors.

Me in the river.

Which Native Americans?

The Seminoles?

The Navajos?

Silver daguerreotype, moving green crypt, current everywhere.

Dive!

It's crazy what you tell yourself just before you take the plunge.

I'm scared of water.

I admit it. I'm scared of water.

Cold shroud.

Live cats in a canvas bag. With a stone.

Forget that.

I see bird shapes, partridges, ptarmigans, pheasants, I see clouds in the background. Oh that's practical, you can stroll through the image. The eye roams, opening voices, a surface that speaks when touched, like those Advent calendars where each day is a new window into little golden events. It's effortless, almost automatic, oh I've got it in my blood you see, and zzzip, I'm there: icy gorse, my eyes shut tight. I leave myself, just like that. If this is being a visionary, it's wonderful, my endorphins send out volleys of happiness.

Just like that.

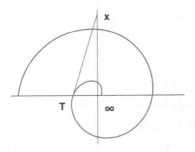

Look at this from above and imagine the point of a pyramid rising toward you.

The drawing turns into something.

An object with volume rising toward infinity.

They used to call this God.

I'm going to join her.

It's not all that hard. Here goes, I'm in, oh it's marvelous. I find a corner, slip between the willows. Pebbles on the right. I see what can be heard. With my fingers I open the words. Walk along the bank with her, in her direction, she agrees, through a meadow without saying a thing, exactly what you wanted, at last we don't need to say "I" anymore. No, sorry, what I meant is that "I" can mean anyone—you, we, they—because I am "I" for once. You know it's rare, I don't regret it, but it's intense, more intense than usual, usually I play a role, terrible, but that's the way it is, out of boredom, etc. I'm developing a very long theory about all that, where in essence I'm outside myself, don't have my own life, etc. and the reasons and causes of all that. She doesn't respond. She's right, no need to talk all the time. And then, talking and walking isn't practical. She's still silent, we walk through an ultrahot garden, buzzing flies, upheaval of dark green trees, grosgrain lace camisole, a countryside at once cultivated and wild. Exactly what you want. Mosaic prairies, enormous heat, longish walk through a jumble of garden, and crackkkk, right up to the house, the perfect house. Normal magic accessible to all. Old England farmstead, library brimming with books, small watercolors of grey rivers, everyday objects engraved in wood, thick beams and the smell of hay, giant cabin on the edge of the forest, I couldn't be happier, I sigh, and kiss her mouth, her neck.

Golden sex.

We steep the afternoon in a wooden bathtub filled with scoops of linden flowers. I like her visual apparatus.

I like her skin and her tendons.

The extraordinary way her nerves articulate her face.

Love in the Sioux way, I say jokingly.

Oh you're a singer.

I didn't know.

Right.

With an axe I chop up a little bonheur-du-jour in violet wood. The inlays look like the precious rosewood and ebony of a violin. I reconstruct. Home-schooled luthier. I glue, cut, no sooner said than done. The two of us put on reductions of cantatas, there's an abandoned harmonium in a corner.

Keys with angel voices.

We peddle to get the little organ breathing.

We think summer, summer from the perspective of winter, we dream summer. We grow and grow, like a heart swelling, arms opening, flood of tears, sternum drop, bumble bee abdomen. I stretch my dragonfly wings. Long live comparisons. Veined tracing paper, silken feather. She makes me think of someone who, without knowing it, imports an enormous landscape into a country scene, pretty but small-scale, like those parks in the middle of cities where they take a few rocks and fast-forward to a mountain chain. Follow her lead, let's grow, take to the seas, abandon the details, vacation time. Gigantic crane, hot-air balloon, drop the sandbags and up we go.

Click! Everything's sharp, like those satellite maps that constantly refresh as you move upward and downward.

Location search.

Zzzzz, the earth takes shape again, joy! Forests fill in, roads stretch out, vegetation spills over. Maybe there's a limit, a focal limit on the camera lens turning in space? Images held in check by the secret service? Not a problem, if you get close enough to the authorized point, everything goes abstract. Censorship? The river becomes a snake of blurry blue in an Amazonia of dark green.

Tachism where the truth ends.

Let's look around for once.

We can see lines.

And cities buried in countryside. Grass covering everything, it's only from way up that you can make out walls. A few hundred yards from where she's bathing, instead of empty fields, a seven-star complex. Marble thermae supplied by the river. Water flows from this enormous spring into subterranean baths.

Huge square pool with mosaics.

Lines of darker grass mark out the foundations. We have the blueprint for the rooms and corridors. I slide past, plunge in. No one's noticed that under this heap of grass lies the tomb of a Roman solder. In the middle of an ordinary field, my friends, the tumulus of a centurion! You walk along, avoiding nettles, concentrate on dodging the barbed wire, until you only see the ground, and craaaack, an unusual contour, a hill too small to be natural. Heads up. But there's nothing to see anymore, and besides, the owner of the field already opened the tombs, just once. Didn't want the Preservation Dept. taking the place by storm. They transform your prairie into a minefield. And the head archeologist barely says hello as he hops from the helicopter.

But these are my tombs.

It leaves one at a loss, you know.

Because they don't want to leave it alone. The next thing's the aqueduct, and that would turn the whole village upside down.

The thermae are under this soccer field, also abandoned.

Twin ruins with cracked cement stands and two rusted, netless goalposts.

Here's the plan view.

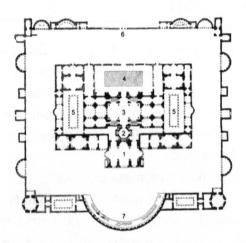

Playing along those lines would change the game. The boys would have to do choreography before scoring a goal. Six-flag corner kick. Home run in togas, touchdown tackle, hunting foxes to mix things up, ball in one hand and razor swipes with the other.

Sword-and-sandal Rollerball.

Any old abandoned tennis court seems like an unexplored site.

Anything has the look of antiquity if you examine it closely.

Like that.

I have no problem living everything at once.

Through squinted eyes, I see only the shape of the players and a black and white halo.

They already had sports fields up here, the only difference was a smaller, buckskin ball filled with the muscles and tendons of animals, hopefully swift.

In the stands, two men discuss a possible return to Rome. We're not too badly off. Same conversation, much later, in the same spot, between English archers after the Hundred Years War.

What if we stayed on, boys?

Gigantic villa, marble complex spanning three hectares, heated pool, spiral staircase carved in the rock so the local pope can slip down unseen to his private hammam.

Immersed in an enormous mauve bathrobe.

Zip, zip, down the steps, elbows pumping.

Chambers of coiling steam.

A labyrinth to doze in and let the dead skin fall.

The warrior's respite.

A retired legionary with his head in a towel fills in his lottery ticket by hand, his wax tablet too soft to use. His right bicep is tattooed with Virgil's *Eclogues*, unabridged.

I am poetry.

Now it's late afternoon and time for an amphora of one-thousand-year-old Armagnac, then a fishing party with the boys. The current mayor of the village gets around on a bright red four-wheeler. Mayor of Bersacum-on-D. I salute you.

Just like that.

When in Rome.

They've diverted the river and spend the days swimming. They've built a stone canal with grates and reservoirs to create waterfalls and keep up a steady flow of huge trout that pass right under your nose as you dine, craacck, sashimi express.

I move along the stone canals.

Mini-lake in a marble basin.

250 m3 per second, on a good day.

What a good idea!

Pass me the soap, Brutus.

I slip from cold to hot, amid a swarm of togas, Hi So-

and-So, Hey You, it's a club, a circle limited to men. I've got a faded red loincloth and a spring green cap, I leap from diving boards at different heights, making figures in the air, slow motion.

Ski jump or swan dive.

A fencing instructor with a spaghetti mustache whips you in the thigh and calls you a peasant for confusing a counter-riposte à temps perdu with a simple disengage.

A mute slave lathers your body with a badger brush after hauling up a bucket of soap, lather, lather, using a little hoist and crying my name: 808 son.

I'm the son of a member.

Nice occupation.

Happily I'm not 666.

I sleep with the window open, the cold valley spread out below me, icy green, angelic, hmmmm, water at 140°, dead skin sloughed off with an ivory spatula like a molting snake, we sit around in terrycloth togas smoking cigars, knocking around ideas—our enterprise, our problems with the new imported slaves and their endless demands, etc., our outrage over the veto on golden parachutes.

Dive!

It's cool.

It's dark.

Hey, I can even read the underwater graffiti.

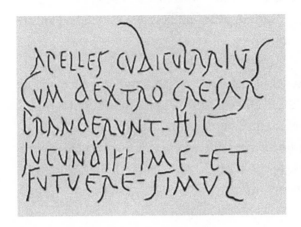

Apelles the valet. Apelles! Not bad for a slave's name. With Dextro, Dexter, imperial slave, dined here most agreeably. Jucundissime? And fucked all the while.

Futuere Simul.

And then in record time, all of that disappeared, the Romans dead, gone, or mixed in with the ex-Gauls, the thermae in ruins and covered with vines.

Only the river remains.

Grandly bearing witness.

To think my cousins find the water disgusting.

All that silt!

And those grasses!

Cesar swam here, girls.

End of the 500s: the last writers with a command of classical Latin die off. A countrified romanic tongue is spoken, with Saxon effects. Our retired centurion feels in Gallic and says what he has to in Latin loaned and borrowed. We put on two or three more fêtes before disappearing like the dinosaurs, dress code: pearl-incrusted sandals, toga bustiere, metal leg warmers. Then it's back to peasantry, good-bye marble, good-bye sun-dried flamingo tongues, good-bye to all those orgies in our laurel wreaths. A few wandering barons start over from scratch: dig a circular pit, dump the earth in the middle and build a cramped wooden castle on the mound. Much later, people will wonder who the artist was that traced the immense circles in the wheat fields.

Slow drain over 1500 years. Radical rural exodus.

Only 1.7% still work the land.

Old Aronde saloons left rusting in front yards, rototillers

broken down and washing machines in the fields.

It's very quickly now.

If I were a historian, I'd write a monograph about this river.

With unpublished documents I'd unearthed, like an image of two men in black on a little road reverently shouldering a mahogany canoe.

Watch for pedestrians.

Photos of a meadow dotted with fragments of pillars and acanthus decorations.

Here the star troubadour is struggling against the current, like a bull.

I'm the hare.

I invent the double-helix sestina.

Welcome to Heaven.

A melancholy old man backstrokes against the current, like a paddle wheeler.

It's all there, I just have to copy it down.

I've got no time to write.

It's faster spoken.

It's better drawn.

There's always tomorrow.

Now let's go back.

And be Gallo-Roman a little while longer.

It's still summer.

We work, we cut hay with long-handled billhooks, we make piles, it's exhausting, the tools are sharp, but it's too hot, no matter how hardened we are, the heat's always a surprise when it's really hot.

River down below. Happily we can swim all the time, eat lunch right here, our legs swinging from the pontoon, berries and cream, warm beer, cold boar. We climb onto the natural platform of moss around the oak tree for a short nap, even the birds sleep, the sun burns each and every field, we have two or three paradoxical dreams. Bugle call, back to work. We're rough, loud, in each other's faces, the dialect is parallel to post-Latin.

Cesar in slang.

But we always patch things up, we hang tarpaulins between the branches, three trestles, and all's well, we eat and drink again, cut hay in the late afternoon, it's cooler now and evening's close, the silence grows, we can hear the quiet things, the first owls, the carps splashing amid the grasses, and night about to fall. The little company decides to head out, spades over shoulders, whistling, and that's when it happens.

Incredible.

An enormous Viking ship passing through the water in

slow motion.

Enormous noise.

Gigantic vessel, armor-plating, barking dogs, guys with braids, Wagnerian helmets, classic red beards, bone piercings, clattering chains. Can you imagine the shock?

Out of near silence. Like that brief moment right before a wound starts to bleed.

Just like that.

Huge noise all of a sudden, like a fighter plane 50 feet overhead as you stand in your yard. A tank charges calmly into the vegetable garden, crushes a row of cabbage and disappears into the alleyway.

A bellowing, an unfamiliar vibration, that's what scares you.

An unlisted noise.

Same for the eyes.

Let's relax.

In the meadow overlooking the water, we'll stretch out on our bellies and take in the scene, reduce the trauma of this image, cut it down to size. The ship is smaller, it's a rowboat, a canoe, replace the horses with a little dachshund growling up in front, two older men, not wearing sports gear or fluorescent vests, something like accidental trappers, metal pot, old canvas scouting packs La Hutte 1934 with leather straps, rowing in silence, the end of the 20th century approaching at top speed.

That's better.

What if I went for a swim now?

How can an old mage like me go swimming? I think. Impossible. Layers upon layers to remove, flannel vest, felt-lined redingote, collar, sock suspenders, pocket watch.

Ff-llllllll, into the water, beard + big white body hitting the silt like a hippo.

I back-float, looking up at the overarching trees, Amazon window, bullseye. Carried by the current, 250 m³ per second, a human raft, moving downstream at the same speed as snakes, spiders and carps. Now gone, under the water, I don't swim laps like an idiot, I'm a dolphin in its stone basin, I move along the edges, scrape my belly against the pebbles on the bottom, like we've been doing since the Neanderthals here, ok? I cry out. Thank you nature, thank you bees, I cry out, thank you world.

I'm not scared at all.

I swim.

I have a mass of ideas, brain making waves.

I think as I swim.

With animals, you never see their dead, a squirrel doesn't lay out his father's corpse in the middle of a path. Whereas you can find an entire family of human beings, group suicide in a park with the Allies closing in, picture-perfect line-up on a bench, ready for a Sunday picnic.

Pleated skirt + cyanide.

A blackbird would never do that.

There's the difference.

Brain making waves.

Let's dive into the wreckage.

Let's get back to our bather.

A rush of images amid the bubbles.

All visionaries swim.

Think it over.
X in the river.
Which river?
Where?
Let's see if we can see.
In Eagles Mere, Pa.

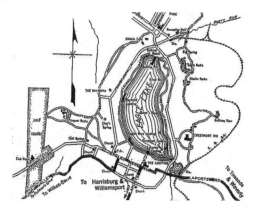

Pa?
Pennsylvania?
Near Allentown. Bethlehem, Loyalsock Forest.
Plenty of fields.
Kind of like here.
That's the hitch, everything's like everything.
It's a real disease.
Mere, Pa?
Mere, *mère*, *maman*, Ma. Pa.
Hey, we're homing in now. Ma, Pa, horse. Smells like
a stable.
Laa—laughing all alone.
Breathe.
You can't laugh and swim at the same time.
Mere, it means pond.
Merely a pond then!

By mere chance, and not merrily. A lake.
No current. I thought it was a river.
I hate lakes.
Dead water.
There are other images.
It's close to?
World's End, State Park.
That's rather nice.
An obscure little spot with such a dramatic name.
There are thousands of images.
Like a circular gallery of paintings 17 miles around.
We place the viewer in the center.
Roll in the story.
It's moving.
The bits of names snap into each other, like the kids' game where you assemble little blocks at the speed of light.

Eagles Mere, that gives us *Eagles* by Brice Marden.
Paintings of intertwining threads.
No comparison.

And that?

That's the Fulmer's.

Henry and Lydia Shaffer Fulmer.

Who are they?

Zide view in witer.

And here's this.

A Remington percussion cap rifle, inlaid with silver studs tracing a deer's head.

Tools, devices, hinged wooden cases for displaying a few stalks of wheat.

A little golden hand clasping a bundle.

Stone baskets overflowing with fruit.

A 6.5-foot rapid action fishing pole with Ulysse IV line and impeccably tapered leader + fly imitating a sudden explosion of Circulaeum-Pandit, creamy pink with translucent wings.

Wicker eel traps.

Portable beehives.

It's all there.

A motherboard.

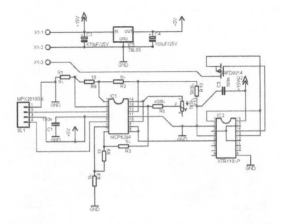

Almost looks like my place.

Being a mage, you know, isn't half bad, I've got the gift of transport.

I'm at home anywhere.

I take whatever shape I want.

Home sweet home, I sleep in a dreamy idea of a bed, patchwork quilt with fabric pieces from an entire family, impeccably sewn, hmmmm, even topstitching, hmmmmm, topstitching.

And that?

Germany, Year Zero.

 I'm moving to everywhere.

I can do all the characters.

Like Kaspar Hauser.

The wild boy.

He's my specialty.

I'm very good at his miraculous arrival by parachute into the village square, letter in hand.

Ich will ein Rei-ter wer-den, I drone.

Ich-will-ein-Reiter-werden.

I want to be a cavalryman, knight, horseman, enter the cavalry. Lancer, Hussar, Uhlan, Dragoon.

That's all I have to say.

A little character on horseback trapped in the ice.

Ich-will-ein-Reiter-werden.

And what's this?

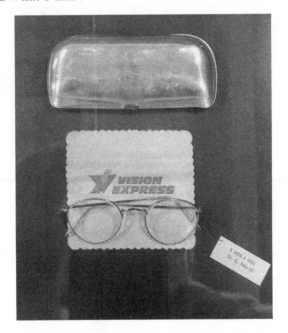

It's restful. Looks like a reliquary.

Legend?

The writing's tiny: glasses of?

Can't quite make out the name, Sewald? Bevall? Harald? Hadorn?

Anon, no, that's "Anonymous."

Adorno?

There's a line in quotes on a piece of yellow paper stuck to the back of the photo: *Imagine Nietzsche playing golf,* and an explanation several paragraphs long.

Wait, it unfolds.

Interesting.

Takes my mind off my own thoughts.

As this lengthy account would have it, whenever Adorno's entourage expressed surprise at finding him in the library of the Grand Hôtel Waldhaus caressing his books, rather than enjoying a little fresh air—and what air!—Adorno is said by his valet to have responded, *Imagine Nietzsche playing golf*, his voice modest, gesturing to his body cramped inside his dark suit, as if to say, I'm unfit—a thinker isn't an athlete, sorry—to those who yelled up the stairs, Theodor! Time for a walk!

You can't ask me to exercise on top of it all. I've given my body over to science. Constant inspiration is exhausting.

And this research!

The images drive you crazy.

Maybe he's wrong, that Adorno, maybe instead of saying, Imagine! as if to say, There's no way, you could mean just the opposite: Imagine Nietzsche playing golf, stated with admiration.

Absolutely! Why not?

Go on, Friedrich, double dare you!

You've got it in the bag.

18 holes in drizzle.

Why I am such a good golfer.

Working on my swing for eternity, I move through the ball toward the horizon. Just like that. Note that I have a special clavicle, shoulder nerve 234B12 linked to the benevolence-heat neuron that fires in one go. Pfiouuuuuffff.

Let's take a moment to relax.

That's how our Friedrich attacks his book, head on. We'll take a leaf from it. *Ich mache mir eine kleine Erleichterung*, copy that down, now there's an expression. You can translate: "I'm granting myself a little respite." Nice way to start a book. Like an ending, after a long series of headaches. *Ich mache mir eine kleine Erleichterung*, write it down again, yes, it literally means... in this *Ich mache mir*, I hear something like: I'm giving this to myself, here. An act that's direct, simple, technical, efficient... automatic, like giving yourself a shot. I don't need anybody, prick. I'm giving myself a kleine little... *Erleichterung:* alleviation, a little alleviation, is that like injecting yourself... with air? Like freeing yourself of a moral weight, like removing a piece of flesh? A prescription for alleviation, woooosh. Let in a little air.

The text doesn't go there.

I'm exaggerating.

I don't read German very well, that's probably why. The text isn't transparent enough, it's sending out signals but refers to another life, it's not clear. Talk about complicated. Like the moron who tries to calculate the roundtrip distance from his finger to the moon. You tell me, Friedrich himself says he's has a disease: he can see language.

In any case, the guy's glowing with health! Bip, I press the button: air. Craack, the little oxygen mask falls from its compartment, fffff. Breathe. Here's a body that works every time. After a long series of headaches. Cured. Let's do the same and be cured.

Phase II.

For all that, you do sense that something's not as relaxed as can be. The guy's at his wits' end. He takes an instant of vacation to start with, but it doesn't last. From the second sentence, he sets out with a vengeance to settle a score in 68 tightly filled pages. Objective: tar and feather a composer.

Wagner.

An eminence who gets smeared, and not only in German. *Wagner est une névrose.*

S'cuse my French.

Not a neurotic, mind you, a neurosis.

That Friedrich, he's a firecracker.

And a good ascendant for a mage.

Maybe I'm his reincarnation.

He's fabulous.

Let's hope he's the one.

I place my hand on the slightly icy page. A liter of ink, herbal sweets, a bottle of elderberry liqueur, and bright sunlight through the window, with the inevitable lake down below.

Marvelous.

The air is superb: 12% humidity, 75°F, sun high, west-west wind.

A fine meteorological body.

Daily urine analysis around 5 pm.

Cuff for monitoring my own blood pressure.

How to self-medicate in 15 lessons.

Why I am such a good student.

Headphones at night to review what you did during the day.

Very good.

Bedroom/study on the third floor with my hostess Caroline von ****, and a regular spot at the dining table.

I could almost go down in slippers.

Another meatball, Herr Professor?

With a few Kartoffeln.

These certainly aren't röstis!

No, they're sliced thin and sautéed, Wien style.

With the bouillon on the side.

Sehr schön.

Gnädige Comptesse.

Kiss on the hand + click of the heels.

Pfiouff, I bust a collar button.

My lodgings are agreeable, the air is invigorating, the food light and easy to digest.

The ideas as well.

I'll write all of this down.

I tidy up my things.

A little round pill box, revolutionary, with its flag, drums and pick motif. One and indivisible.

Ach the Republic!

With those big elephant tranquilizers inside the box.

Gulp.

I've finished *The Case of Wagner*, I'm well into *Ecce Homo*, just two or three final chapters that I can toss off in a week.

I'll get started tomorrow morning.

That's it, I've become who I already am.

I have the body of my ideas.

I mime, sustain, envisage, play, disembody, interpret, represent, and illustrate them.

A famous philosopher becomes a golf champion and doesn't end up crazy.

I'm going to play old school.

Hit it straight down the middle.

Like the boys who invented the game on the edge of the Scottish cliffs.

You need a very clever dog to find a ball in the heather 800 misty yards away.

Why I am such a good dog.

I'm going to send one flying beyond the cliffs and land it on the heath, piouf. Nowadays, some guys play from building to building.

Third hole atop the Empire State Building.

Philosophizing with a club.

Laa-laa-laa.

It's a bad sign to laugh all alone.

The beginning of those headaches.

I'm going to end up with my arms around a horse's neck. Stop.

I tidy up my desk to get a jump on my new life so I can start bright and early tomorrow morning becoming who I really am already.

As simple as that.

I'm so skilled at tidying up.

I use small cloths with a gentle abrasive action to clean the various lenses I look through daily, a folding loupe to examine letters, my eyeglasses, and a little telescope, not to spy on Jupiter but to observe the meadows, to magnify a stalk of wheat a few miles away. You can see the parasites darting about on a leaf. I polish the rings of pens and the little spring-mounted silver hand, ancestor of the Boston clip No. 1 which I possess in great number. Like those bits of colored tape, piled in the form of a coral snake. I wax the pencil cases. I apply Miror to the copper boxes. Here's where I keep the black-edged calling cards for mourning, not so useful anymore since I've no one left to lose. Lightly coated 105g paper you can slide rapidly between blocks of apparently separate things on the page.

Become who you are.

Like that.

Bedtime.

2

A canopy bed is ideal, a kind of container where you can forget everything. Bad thoughts, surplus phrases burning in your memory, you sweep them up and send them whirring through the meanders of the brain. This merry-go-round saves my life. Every morning, rain or shine, I struggle, and God knows how complicated it is with this system of sheets, quilts, coverlets, pillows and the step-by-step, obligatory circuit that anxiety must take to dissolve away, I struggle, I torture myself to find out whether happiness is possible. Or approximative happiness. People used to sleep sitting up. Smart. So as not to lose their place in the conversation. To stay in the loop, to avoid leaving their seat in circles, families, assemblies, trials, waiting rooms, so as not to disappear, person and property, to a bed every night, almost to the dead. But that was long ago, things are totally different now, we've become used to lying down, it's good for you, sleep is good, you stretch out and the night takes you. Like woodcutters attacking a tree from different angles, sinking their axes deeper and deeper until the trunk is barely a thread, you fall asleep for an instant, dream pilot burning, a little steam engine deep in the forest, steam, transmission. Let's consider this energy that resembles a plant's. Organism idea, shape problem. At one time, after a long period of nocturnal hallucinations, I suffered from a terrible pain in my stomach, every morning, at dawn, rain or shine, a knot of anxiety, of nerves, of aggressive foreign flesh. And then one day, just like that, ffft, miraculously, you probe yourself, incredulous. It's gone. Finished. Snap, and in a snap of the fingers, you retrospectively realize everything you've been through, you understand that the thing hurting you was also hurting itself. The pain was an organ and this organ the pain. Like that old trick of a missing arm you still feel, its sudden absence is what reveals everything about it. Poof, and you have proof of existence. That's good. I'll use it again when the time comes.

In short, it works, I'm light as air! Everything's fine. I'm basically a machine. So much the better, I can just listen to the body breathing, all by itself. Breathe, breathe.

To keep watch over a body, you need a parlor without heat. Candle. Cigar. My psalms. And only one sound: me breathing like this, brea, brea. Condensation. Fffff. I breathe. A body manifests itself with mist.

Breathe.

It's a time to be resuscitated.

I can see images, as easily as a man who, to pass the time as he lies in bed, hoping for the arrival of someone he desires furiously, listens to the elevator's abrupt stops, hoping this'll be it, his floor, no, one floor up, wait, he deciphers the dull clank of metal and the clatter of the pulleys, accompanied by a sudden surge from the heater through the pipes, a tunnel of sounds through the apartment, and what music! Ultracold, harsh, repetitive, creaks + cries, and to ease his mind, decides to run his memories along his windowpanes, as easily as if he had a magic lantern, or one of those wooden boxes you use to look at photographs on glass in three dimensions. A mental View-Master! Collected images of your loved one! exclaims the manual. Against the backdrop of beaches, rivers, prairies, skyscrapers. Anything you want. Slip your head through the neck hole of the carnival sailor, the monster, it's effortless, life-changing. It works. Music! I'm in the middle of a machine, I've blown up my brain to the size of my room. Silence. I listen religiously to the sounds of my bed like someone who decides to invite a string quartet to play Beethoven's 15th in the hallway.

Surround sound.

Amazing.

But it has nothing to do with Beethoven anymore.

Around me, in the drawers, are heaps of hodgepodge, small useless objects to be kept just in case: copper wall-mounts to hold the tiebacks if the curtains are ever re-hung, parasol clip, mismatched playing cards, sturdy thread to sew on buttons or repair a seal-skin tunic, ribbons and wrapping paper to discreetly recycle a gift, a rusty valve, marker caps, bits of pumice stone, forgotten jelly beans agglutinated into a sold chunk, the debris of things turned into involuntary treasure. And the time spent trying to think of how you might use all these unrelated things leaves you speechless, each novel combination calls up a scene. Unclip the parasol and summer opens wide.

While the Scotch tape keeps the ice caps in place.

You leave things to age involuntarily in an attic cemetery or a drawer, or an isolated cabinet installed in an entryway and occasionally filled with these abandoned but keepable things. Like the wooden egg for darning socks.

Keep it.

Because the worn wood has a patina you'd miss if you didn't? Like the very old staircase you set out to strip one day where millions of steps have left their mark. You can follow the exact trajectory of people climbing and calculate the ballistics of the bodies who have charged up the stairs since Christopher Columbus.

Reproduce *that* in a factory!

Objects exiled to drawers, but also to the plastic or

stoneware or metal receptacle, a kind of rigid basket found in every kitchen, where poor orphaned and lost objects mingle, like bodies tenderly exchanging their molecules and losing themselves into life and death, corks, oven manuals in Norwegian, orange ballpoints without a point, the bright pink hinge of a child's flip phone, lavender debris, a series of mismatched screws, nativity statuettes and their decapitated heads.

The objects are transported by the person kind enough to play the mother in a space X, generally in the kangaroo pocket of an apron or sweat suit, the Good Enough Mother's indoor uniform, and craaack, pocket contents transferred to drawer. And in the end, it's the only thing that'll remain of the life operation of a family or group. The couch: sold, clothes and shoes tossed into heavy-duty garbage bags, so all that's left, when everybody's gone, are the squares of dust on the walls where pictures once hung, and cardboard boxes of wreckage, fallout from breakdown or burnout, bits of things busted, or semi-precious, a jade dance card, a silk ribbon wrapped around a little ivory barrel with a brass crank, so you have the option of measuring a room in either feet or cubits.

I'm surrounded by useless tools.

A real mishmash.

What to do?

An agglutination of vestiges from different eras, a private historical dump.

A rusted 9-volt battery next to a book on maritime law threatening to crush a fragment of light fixture lying underneath.

My brain is… cluttered.

No, that's not it.

Wrong adjective.

Wrong image.

I need to find the image of Lord Carnavon entering King Tut's tomb.

There's been a break-in.

Someone steals into your house, turns things upside down and immediately bars access for five centuries.

That image?

No.

There's another one, where you see two gods with cat-heads on either side of a smashed chariot.

My brain's more like that.

Pretty banal, really.

You see it everywhere, in a field where people have abandoned washing machines and broken mirrors, poor indoor objects left out in the open air, or in the streets, floral paper still stuck to the wall of a demolished building.

Chimneys left hanging.

A playroom in mid-air.

But it's okay.

I'm a real Robinson.

I know how to handle a tricky situation.

You can run into trouble anywhere.

No need for a desert island.

Take a modern train station, you still find intractable pieces of wood embedded in the cement.

Like that.

It's weird to find this archaic stop where an ultra-modern train pulls in.

Maybe to prevent the worst possible accident, like a runaway train at full speed, the old methods are still best.

When it's Life or Death, you go with the old stuff, a barrel-maker's technique, heat the wood after you put the hoops on.

Hardened with an absorptive effect.

All the same, it's odd.

It's like a modern car still having a long rusty rod with a spring clamp, the kind they used on carriages, the only brake capable of stopping a big four-door on a slope.

Crouink.

What a mix!

Same story with these plastic tubes they drive into the foot of trees planted along a street, to send water under the asphalt during the first years of growth, forgotten after that, stuck to the child-tree forever like a crushed baby bottle.

Look at that.

The roots will mesh with it, like wisteria wraps around electric cables and pipes deep underground, a new plastic plant.

What a mishmash.

Wrinkly things, balls of things, and ?

Same with the old stagecoach road, all that remains are a dozen sloping feet at the place where people got attacked.

What a mix.

The landscape is dense.

I suddenly notice the little black spot at the top of the secretary. And the same thing one level down. You could really almost say one floor down, because this huge piece of furniture resembles a little house or a columned temple in dark wood. The same spot twice, vertically aligned, is no ink spot.

A trace of something?

I don't know, could be something that burnt. The path of a flame. A candle set in the same place every day, an overheated gas lamp, slow burn or sudden accident, you can't really tell. In any case, someone sat here before I did.

I realize this slowly.

Such a discovery is rare with old furniture, their patina makes everything relative. A series of slip-ups, a succession of impacts, an infinity of daily brutalities forgotten in the wax. Scratches, water droplets, bore holes, everything's gone.

Repressed drama.

These are bore holes.

It's now known that during mating, woodborers call each other regularly at the same time, hitting their heads against the wood. Can't hear a thing anymore.

Using an old desk blotter, I discover a skein of lines on the back, engraved from a fountain pen, a series of phrases, cross-outs and additions in every direction, compressed. Superposition of: Sincerely yours, on: Yours in friendship,

on: I remain your most humble, barred. Like that. Help me.
Julien.

Send clothing.

Urgent.

Cross-outs.

Broke.

Hurry.

Cross-outs.

Oh dear sister.

Cross-outs.

Thank you for the apricots. And the trousers. Hurry. Your brother from afar. Ex-voto engraved in the blotter. I imagine raised contours on these little surviving stumps of sentence, I give them depth, see the hands darting as they trace out declarations, death announcements, household accounts, requests for money and love, all of that now a Rosetta Stone. At one time, people wrote this way to save space.

How could you re-establish space and depth between

these lines?

A 3D search?

I read somewhere that people today buy their tools ready-to-use, a relatively new development in history.

Do they all exist, carefully arranged in a warehouse, waiting for me?

Is it possible to make a unique tool for just one person's use?

Answer me!

Is there a tool that can measure the wear on paving stones from people passing through a space X over two centuries?

No answer.

But let's not give up at the slightest obstacle.

I do have everything I need here.

Really can't complain.

Everything's available.

It's as if I had access to gigantic hangars bursting with documents, metal shelves, a small crank, you can move the walls of the archives forward and back at will.

But in a modern version.

They used to search through all of that on roller-skates, ffff-ffff, 1922, 1870, 1390, back through time.

Just like that.

Now, it's within easy reach.

Voice controls.

Touch any word and a door opens onto explanatory texts.

I compress myself.

Decompress myself.

A new sport.

That's what the manual keeps obsessing over.

Annex of an annex of an annex.

As if someone had compiled information on the protagonists in the margins. Maps of the locations, dialogues written in white pen on photographs. Technical notes as well. Accompanied by geopolitical notes, with charts and maps.

War letters.

Farm accounts.

Museum inventories.

And drawings.

Someone struggling to explain decides to draw a diagram.

Just like that.

You take someone by surprise in the middle of a thought.

Dive headlong into the lisp of life.

The history of the world in paste-ups and run-offs.

Someone decides to capture the history of the world since God until almost now on a single sheet of paper.

Looks a bit like a tree.

The scenarios condense.

And they do talk a lot about trees.

Can you see that one, way in the back?

A linden, planted in 1848.

Something's written on it.

Freedom tree.

And the names of the guys who dug the hole and planted the tree. Along with everything else. The invoices, the yelling when the tree died, how they pulled up the roots.

A letter from the pruner.

Involuntary poem.

Sorry.

I made.

A mistake.

Cut a little too.
Sorry about the chestnut, etc.
Lots of tree stories.
A treatise on the silver linden.

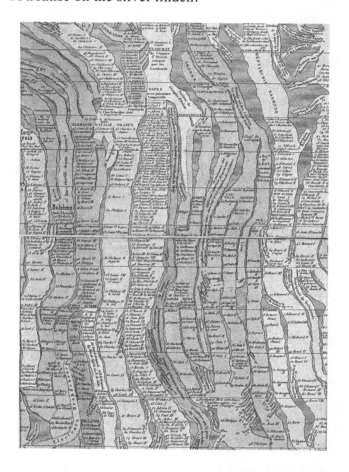

A very sad tome on the extinction of the elm.

Drawings of branching points, ideal arbor pruning, ah! Upside down it looks like a body, with two thighs.

And sex at the fold.

Magnificent.

Ahhh, I have everything here.

What comfort!

Big tables where you can spread out the documents.

A set of magnifying glasses to get down to details.

Microscopes to analyze the ink.

The latest model of a carbon-14 dating device, with automatic correction and a new "Old Wood Effect" function.

Gets obsolete fast, this equipment.

First-hand accounts.

And all of it passed down orally. Absolutely.

Re-transcribed word for word.

You can zoom in or out, like in the days of the microfiche reader, all in the blink of an eye.

Can't complain at all.

Not just Gallo-Roman—modern, too!

Seems exactly like a real forest, you could even get lost in there, hey this tree looks like the one I just saw, we're crossing the same clearing, but at another angle, advantage: stumble right onto anything, follow up any path, dive in immediately, one life links into the next, jump back, turn around, start over. I spend so much of my life in this library of memories I'll end up buried alive like those people who make hallways through giant stacks of newspapers. A cathedral in a dumpster. You'll recall the guy who, in a building since bombed out, accumulated a collage that grew inexorably, as if it were alive, so he rented the upstairs apartment and broke through the ceiling to continue adding to the sculpture. I really get that. You end up with intriguing mixtures. Shoes melted onto a jade necklace and a box of nails, skull and crossbones incrusted with diamonds, cassette recorder in smithereens welded to a kid's steam engine for demonstrating the importance of the industrial revolution. Original letters glued onto maps and graphs. Scientific images along the contours of graffiti, passport stamps covering aboriginal pornography, Christmas decorations. Stop.

Burn it.

Douse the whole thing with gasoline.

Or do what one countess did when she gave the keys of the château library to a surrealist painter armed with a cutter.

Let's take this bit of De Vinci and glue it on this *Life* photograph.

It'll cost you.

But you gain space.

A mage?

Why'd I say that?

I'm not a mage at all.

What's going on?

Why would I be a mage?

I'm being influenced.

Must be coming from somewhere.

Let's do a search.

I've got to have a biography somewhere.

A search with my name.

You come up with Poltrot, Moulin de Poltrot, a place name, a first name, Poltrot de Méré, the one who assassinated the Duc de Guise.

Off to a great start.

Photo of a razed castle, collapsed minidungeon in the woods with gigantic oaks towering over the stones.

What's unusual is that the castle was in a hole, standing defenseless in a loop of black river. Looks like a small abandoned planet.

This guy Poltrot was carefully cut into pieces and exposed on the Place de Grève in Paris.

Quarters of the hero's meat.

We're gaining ground in every direction.

A series of destinies online.

A list of screw-ups.

Florian and Florida, twins drowned in the river.

Daguerreotype.

It's rolling.

Departure for Valmy on foot.

A penniless band of patriots.

Disappearance in Salamanca. Someone loses a leg crossing the Elbe. A man takes up arms in 1830, is appointed prefect, goes mad, rents four apartments in Paris to go out incognito and forgets his family, broke and in rags, at the far end of a remote valley.

Watercolors.

Letters.

Litigation.

Tables.

Application forms.

An émigré during the Revolution never returns from exile, his cousin, a deputy for the third estate, calls for his execution.

Declaration.

Accounts.

Bills.

Contracts.

A physician-philosopher heads into the woods to meet Malebranche. And gets lost.

Photos.

Photos.

Speeding ticket.

A plantation owner is burned in Saint-Domingue. A spy for Louis XV keeps an eye on the protestants in Geneva and sleeps with Rousseau's mother.

Confessions.

Data sheets.

A native of Versailles and *ex-pacificateur* in Algeria shoots his brother Anatole, a Communard.

Engraving.

No, he stops just short of shooting him, phew!

Anatole collected old copies of *Père Duchêne* in color.

An ex-1848-revolutionary sleeps with Napoleon III, a young Croix-de-Feu rushes to Vichy. A WWI mutineer ends up bureau chef at the National Police. A Trotskyite becomes a state prosecutor, etc.

Images.

Images.

And nearly all of them from the top of the heap, on the side of might. Something's about to give.

Photo.

Scans.

Testimony.

Ration card.

Safe conduct pass.

A family's store of ordinary dreams comes crashing down. All it takes is the occasional Frankenstein.

A mage!

Found him.

On the left side of the tree.

In a corner.

A great-uncle by marriage, not too far removed.
Maybe I have his DNA.
That's it!
It's tempting.
The role model I've been searching for.
He must be my real ancestor.
Fame and glory.
What do you want to be one day?
A mage.
You can picture the young man, who's maybe a little ambitious.
In uniform!
Photos.
Photos.
And the groupies are so very enthusiastic.
Photos.
Black magic séances on opium.
Photos.
A little jail time to harden up.
Code name: Eliphas Lévi.
Painting.
First appearance as Grand Master, of what I don't know.
Enormous beard and oriental cap.
Armored Gothic bureau and stuffed crows.
Pretty hellish.
Anecdotes.
His wedding lunch on the Pont-Neuf bridge.
Just enough money for two paper cones of frites.
Defrocked priest, 1848 revolutionary, initiator of occultism.
Balzac penned his portrait.

The quest for the absolute.

Hugo called on him looking for Adèle.

This way, Victor.

Rimbaud copied him.

Breton kept his picture on his nightstand between a shrunken head and a voodoo mummy.

Mick Jagger recited him backward.

Did I mention the books?

Here's a guy who took the trouble to write.

Thousands of pages.

About what?

This science will cast a new light on the philosophy of history and will serve as a synthesis of all the natural sciences. The law of balanced forces and organic compensations will renew physics and chemistry; from one discovery to the next, we will return to a hermetic philosophy, admiring its prodigious simplicity and clarity, forgotten all these many years...

Okay.

...Philosophy will be as exact as mathematics...

Really!

...True ideas, those synonymous with being and constituting the science of reality, are akin to reason and justice, in that their proportions are exact and their equations rigorous, like numbers...

Perfect.

...Thus error will only be possible in ignorance; real knowledge will no longer err...

And while you're at it...

...Esthetics will no longer be subject to the whims of taste, which change as fashion changes...

Good news.

...If beauty is the splendor of truth, infallible calculations must be performed on the rays of any light, whose source will be known incontestably and determined with rigorous precision...

Whoa.

...Poetry will lose its wild, subversive tendencies. Poets will no longer be the dangerous enchanters whom Plato banished from his Republic after crowning them with flowers; they will be the musicians of reason and the gracious mathematicians of harmony...

Beautiful idea.

...Is this to say that the Earth will become an Eldorado? No, for as long as humanity exists, there will always be children, which is to say the weak, the small, the ignorant and the poor...

Ouch.

...But society will be governed by its true masters...

Can't say I'm surprised.

...And there will be no evil in human life that cannot be rectified. We will realize that divine miracles are eternal, and we will no longer worship the phantoms of the imagination, basing our beliefs on unexplained marvels. The strangeness of a phenomenon only proves our ignorance of the laws of nature. When God wants to make himself known to us, he enlightens our rational mind rather than seeking to confuse or surprise us.

And I suppose I have to look like this.

No way.

I suppose I have to draw pentagrams all day.

Combine the Tarot with Kabbalah.

Whoa.

I suppose I have to ponder joining the Trappists, traveling across France with an itinerant actor friend, reading 20,000 volumes in an abbey, spending eight months in jail with Lamennais, publishing a *Book of Tears*, crossing paths with the ghost of Apollonius de Tyana, dining tête-à-tête with Jean-Marie Ragon, giving private lessons in politics, having recurrent bouts of bronchitis, abandoning Flora Tristan, leaving a mother to poison herself with gas, attending meetings of the Loge du Parfait Silence, writing one thousand letters to an Italian baron, and dying of elephantiasis.

There are some things I don't know how to do.

You tell me that at the beginning of the 21st century, Eliphas Lévi was the name of a Japanese punk band whose last song starts with

ai nana no higeki akai meikyuu

This is getting complicated.

And what about this guy?

Look at his hat!

Must have had an understanding hat-maker.

What's most important is clothing, the day after a revolution the seamstress is already swamped. Eliphas's wife was admitted into the first club of feminists. Make me a dress for a Vesuvian. Add a little red piping to this butterfly-wing lining in blue.

And the last fight let us face.

I wear my opinions.

In any case, it's a weird hat.

Later he'd opt for a leather fez, D'Annunzio style, fascist sport.

A bit more run-of-the-mill.

Like the hussar housecoat, just so visitors won't think you live in a trailer.

The man in the pointed hat is Aleister Crowley, Eliphas's descendant, no, not his descendant, his reincarnation, born the day he died.

May 31, 1875.

Helps.

Mage II, Mage III in fact, given that our Eliphas was supposedly the descendent of Rabelais, not the descendent, but "Rabelais himself."

It's spelled out.

In black and white.

I'm Rabelais.

Might as well be.

In any case, number III pushed the envelope a bit.

With this business about The Hermetic Order of the Golden Dawn.

And the Beast, 666, that stuff.

Hi there, I'm the devil.

The guy started young, while still at Trinity College, dressing up in red, wearing horns.

Hello.

This is my cousin.

He ended up believing it all.

Here he is as Grand Master of the Order, next to him, Mussolini looks like an accountant.

Photos.

Final act: torture-fuck fests in an Italian villa. The Inventor of Sexual Magic. A cult, it turns out, is key to sexual success. There was also the little interlude with the MI5, being mixed up with the German secret service, giving Himmler a hand at Burg, the refurbished castle for training the SS in occultism. The boys had to meditate in medieval cells, 6 months.

Recordings.

Super 8.

Polaroid.

Fortifies the youth.

Candle, knout, and bonfire.

I'm having a solid silver brooch made with a German shepherd motif.

It'll all end in 2040 at some split-level with a faux stone exterior. Weekend fisting on All Saint's Day, hosted by a Satanist couple.

Color brochure.

On Halloween night, Cathy's making beef Burgundy.

Here, try on this mask of Tezcatlipoca.

Hey there, it's me!

And that?

I can't look at that.

My eyes are closed.

A goat-devil drawing.

If I'm scared, that means I'm not a mage.

Yipes.

Whew.

No more searches.

We've collected a few facts, more or less remarkable, but what links them all together leads straight to hell.

Before you can say "Jack Robinson."

48 to 42 at top speed.

And not 42 BC, 1942.

From the revolutionary left to far beyond the right.

Have a nice vacation.

And that? Wronski's prognometer, a mathematico-philosophical machine that, according to a specialist, Eliphas had the luck to discover one day at an antiquary's, this machine was supposed to calculate the probabilities of present, past and future facts, in order to determine the value of all *imaginable x's*.

I'd need the manual.

Apparently this machine is with the descendants of Papus, alias Gérard Encausse, a mage from another branch.

Greetings, Gérard.

Today there are geraniums instead of skulls in this apartment.

We've kept you a room.

I don't want to reincarnate as anybody or be anybody's reincarnation.

We're free after all.

This is not some horror flick where a woman with a bird head gives birth to the devil in person.

A devil in diapers.

I'm not a mage.

I don't give a damn about the family.

You're only a mage if you decide to be.

Magi can choose to be the descendent of anyone, but I'm not interested.

Reverse adoption.

The child's name kept sealed.

The risk is that some nutcase reincarnates as you without warning.

But you're dead already, phew.

A series of people plunge into one another, each devouring the next. I'm the flesh of the serpent eaten by the serpent. Just like that, I'm eternal.

What a nightmare.

No chance of that happening to me. I said mage, like that, for something to say. I'm not a visionary at all, I lied, confession: I work hard, I've got no special gifts. I'm ordinary. Everything I do is pieced together. Line after line. And then, fortunately, you don't reincarnate within the same family. The fact that my grand-uncle's a mage is the very reason I don't run the risk of becoming one, I just had to think about it.

I'm dancing.

I'm free.

I dance all alone as if ten thousand people danced with me.

Parquet floor and open sky.

Phhhew.

Unless someone's put a curse on me.

I can't believe that, just this morning I received an invitation in the mail to participate in an artistic project, photos of a smashed cat, pancake of dark fur transported in a garbage bag. Someone nails a raven to the barn door to send you into a tailspin.

Of course not.

At least, I hope not.

Besides, they're going to publish my refusal letter in a real artist's catalog.

I don't have time to write.

Phhhew. This is real life.

We've gained centuries.

I'm dancing.

I dance with the amplified music of my body.

I'm positive.

One by one, I remove all the bad thoughts, I translate them into flesh one by one, calmly I transplant, I balance my organs, feel the cogs, I think in volume and in mass, in fluids, in fleets of atoms, my soul's the shape of a heart.

With arteries like an octopus.

All images are true.

Besides, if I'd wanted to be a mage, I should have looked

for my model elsewhere, like the Barambaras, who have to marry in the group BN/987-TY, as opposite as possible to you.

Outside of the tree.

Diagonally through the branches.

Must have fresh blood.

Zero risk for me.

Everything's fine.

This series of reincarnations is so tiring, it has to stop, why make everything so difficult? Constant responsibility, I've got to be a living, breathing temple in their memory, it's exhausting.

A mage can't stop being a mage.

Horrible.

People are weird, I can take a break, can't I? Not a chance, you have to be professional. Deliver every time. A pro at something you foisted on a hostile family, against all odds. Now that you've convinced them, they demand results.

The Nobel Prize of magi!

The Medal of Honor in occultism!

Mr. Flow of the Year!

Get cracking, mage.

Even as a serial killer I'd have to pick up the pace so I could be Number 1 somewhere. The guy who liquidated the most redheads in Arizona over ten years.

Bravo son.

But no one's asking me for that.

I wasn't "appointed."

Or self-appointed, for that matter.

I wasn't approached by the brothers.

I've got nothing to do with any of that.

I don't have a master.

I played at being a slave to understand how masters were slaves, and thus masters, as slaves of their masters, and the same thing in reverse.

Just for the investigation.

I've never been on an island.

I'm not a carpenter.

Or a saint.

Or a survivor.

These are images.

I project myself.

I hate mythology, ancient Greek drama, masks, shouting back and forth, carnivals, agoras, forums.

I hate groups.

I've chosen the only myth where the hero is truly alone.

On vacation.

I'm not crazy.

I'm outside of the lineage.

I'm an orphan and fine.

Later.

I'm not engraved in stone.

I'm not a character.

I'm a fraction of moment of matter.

A little machine.

Containing other machines ad infinitum.

Nothing magical in that.

I fall into rank with the cells.

Left, left, left right left.

I'm a quark.

My hadrons gallop.

They belong to the world and everyone in it.

I'm happy.
This thing lives and breathes.
It works.
I swim so much my feet web.
I dance so much my hands fan.
I'm evolving.
Fifty drawings to murder magic.
Oh thank you *****.
Let's forget whoever I come from, I'm on vacation.
The night's cool, there are cicadas. There's an icy wind that deeply refreshes our organs. I relax. In the middle of the enormous heat. I relax. Nighttime.
Summertime, I like summer.
And now, bedtime.

Okay, one more.

Bizardel, Bizardel?

The first author I met wrote a who's who: *Bottin des Américains à Paris pendant la Révolution.*

We're a few steps away from my own childhood.

This thing runs on its own.

You can't stop a search just like that.

It's like when you're angry.

There's no going back.

I dial Alma 3456.

Nothing.

Carnot 6789?

No answer.

I let it ring in the silence for a long time.

Pigalle 7007?

Ah.

You can hear voices.

It's incredible.

I really do have flow.

I've got gifts.

Sounds like a recording… a dinner recording.

Does that exist?

A pirated family drama?

On a disk where you hear people around an Easter ham ripping each other apart. Someone planted a microphone under the table.

In the flowers.

Definitely.

It's in the flowers every time.

A single copy of a homemade radio drama, there is such a thing, you can readily find them in abandoned boxes, after a move, forgotten in the cellar. Dusty old cassettes, in a format no one'll ever be able to read, chipped diskette, flash drive full of jelly.

Millions of words lost to the ether.

Like Nixon talking to himself.

Watergate tapes in the attic.

Insults.

It doesn't work. What you need are images, even if they're as round and blurry as what you see through a door's peephole.

Like this.

Amateur theater performance, says the legend.

Only seen through a mouse hole.

Something like that... floaty beings in gray, paper walls with a gray reserve, flashed through with light, long-exposure painting, a lemon levitating.

A flash of fire.

When you can't see anything, you hear all the better, the words stand out better in the dark, it's clear. I see shapes... like in a game of blind man's bluff where you're cheating a little.

You identify bodies, feel the outlines of things moving, click of beads, whiff of leather, perfumed Duc carriage and cadaverine, horse's rump, pig's foot, etc.

Ocean liner, family, billowing smoke.

Let's get a little closer.

Zero risk.

You end up seeing faces.

Things sharpen up as fast as a sculptor fashions an arm from a mound of clay.

6, rue de Liège.

What became of the apartment after we left.

The owner, Marquise de C., a descendant of the military architect Vauban, which helps when you're defending your property, claimed she had to move her children in and kicked us out. Well and good. Then just 30 years later I learn from an old high-school friend that her children didn't quite… live there.

They transformed the place into a theater.

Stupefaction!

Aside: our replacements were the La Forest-Divonnes. What a pretty surname, like Stermaria, which contains within it the lens of the Lake and the mist of the woods and this gentle way of recounting, I read that somewhere, but still.

To transform an apartment into a theater.

Our apartment!

Honestly.

My sister's room the wings of a Chekhov play.

The living room a stage!

The dining room a wardrobe.

What a weird life in place of my own.

In the same building: first floor, studio of the marquise's sculptor brother. For a human-sized statue of Saint Christopher, and in exchange for candy, pose held, perched on the shoulders of a half-naked bearded man, the ground covered with a plastic tarp to represent the waves.

Here's the central point.

The primitive scene.

If there absolutely has to be one.

The smell of clay, the hulk's hairy shoulders, me as

Jesus lugged around unawares, and if you cut vertically through the scene, it's exactly three floors below my parent's bedroom.

My life's user manual.

Something medical, religious, grave, and empty in one scene.

My fate as a statue.

Think it over.

Auto-biomagical.

Marquise de C., C. stands for Chérizy.

Chère Marquise de Chérizy, Dear Marquise de Chérizy.

A loving family name.

Let's do a search.

And in two seconds we find her offspring masterminding the Priory of Sion hoax in the 1960s.

False Templar documents.

More magi!

We can't escape.

Light a match.

Autodafé!

Auto-whatever-you-say!

Autoterrorist.

I'm going to blow myself up at the same time.

Martyr.

There's a good character for you!

Now.

And just as I'm about to light the gasoline-soaked furniture on fire, I hear a man climbing the stairs, still young, coming back from the circle.

Whistling.

Down at the bottom of the stairs, you can see the

chandelier held by the stone woman like a rocket on its launching pad.

Before blast-off.

Before the bombs.

I saw Morand eating a hard-boiled egg and drinking a Coke at the Bar de l'Auto. He did an imitation of Proust going home at night, my father told me, slamming the door behind him, and he started to do the other guy's voice, who was imitating the other guy.

The man who talked to the man who talked to the bear.

And then muffled howls as if families were wolves or other more complex animals.

Goat hyena.

Warthog rat.

Golden-eyed zander on a Persian rug.

A line stretched taut in the dark.

I make a hole in the parquet like an Eskimo cutting the ice.

The river below.

A watchtower on the water.

Wood and stone.

The black water roars.

Dark shaft room.

Oh, frozen island of the night.

I lower an interline fishing rod.

I'm on the verge of tears.

I catch an enormous fish.

Flaming torch.

Green scales in black water.

I fish in my catacombs.

Tears.

I'll never kill a fish again.

Tears.

Tears.

Tears.

Tears.

Tears.

This bed is miraculous.

Bright and early, it morphs into a desk, in the blink of an eye, only one of the sides is a curtain, the other three are wooden panels. A lustrous black box, filled with shelves at different heights and depths, fold-out boards and insertable leaves. Cookies are prepared in an iron distributor, always crunchy and available, a little thermos of coffee.

I'm ready.

Let's end the Terror.

And get cracking.

Otherwise, what good is this comfort?

Only an idiot lets a factory sleep.

If I'm a happy machine, let's step on it.

Since nothing gets outmoded faster than modern tools. Look at the shit-brown plastic of a Boeing's molded cabin, the Star Wars laptops. Wiring invades electronic ex-cathedrals.

Let's go.

The temperature of the comforter is perfect, it's still night in the morning, the pillow's curve follows the shape of my skull, the adjustable lamp throws a circle on the white sheet, I grab a volume from a row of unread books.

The correspondence of Alfred de Vigny.

Vigny? That's weird, let's take a closer look. I glue my eye to the pages. I get inside the text, I read vertically. Something new. I cut half of the lines, they fall into place, making little blocks with enormous letters in a blurry frame, vertigo around a hand glass.

I realize you were
dreading
—Something
Cut.
All paths
today

100

to your heart
Cut.
In my own
all of this for me, and thus
Cut.
Tenderness! thus I, not your—
For me—your consola-
Cut.
You named it so and I
Cough and smile, dreaming
Our secret life
—no matter how
writing to match the movements
Cut.
When
love
Cut.
My angel I send you kisses
here
Cut.
The night the skin
breathe
Stop.

I open my eyes again just as the big curtain slides past. The dark room fills with a developing bath. The immense and central canopy bed that contains me is itself surrounded by an orange curtain and, happily, soft light inside, an illuminated orange hue, orange sunlight, hmmmm, I glide through a slit, black mahogany tray with fold-out legs, like a little desk for the bedridden, I'm my own servant, you always are, more or less, when you're on a desert island all alone. I'm turning into an idiot. If you please, Sir, six soft-boiled eggs at 15-second cooking intervals, depending on the size of each egg. Since in this pre-industrial country, egg size is not standardized, I say to myself, I'm white as a sheet, I should eat a dozen.

Coffee in a portable glass alembic, elegant and interminable.

Long, thin strips of toast dusted with fleur de sel. Carafe of orange juice the color of the curtains. And I dictate my

First night poem

I realize you were dreading, good, from the right side, justified on your machine

like that
I realize you were dreading

That's it.

Like a word that leaves late and runs straight into a wall, sigh, and we're off again, like clearing your throat, hyphen, upper-case S, to take a big swing, at something, then

—Something
all paths
today
to your heart

Like a little list, crack, falls short of the end, all paths / today / to your heart, there, white space and begin at exactly the same spot with

In my own

To your heart […] in my own, hmmm, nice, isn't it?
Not bad.
Literature's not so bad.
It's a solution for getting a handle on things.
I position the four steps so I can get down from the bed,

whhhew, it's night again, hmmmm, I wrap a thick robe over my suit. The diffuse electric light takes nothing away from the old-fashioned glow of the candlesticks.

Come on, let's go, I turn around the table dictating, arms crossed, we're making the Master's Book, boom boom boom, and you, with your pallor, your apple green redingote, sharpen that pencil and make it scratch.

I listen to myself.

We've set up Biedermeier furniture, little interiors of cathedrals framed in black, we turn down the heat, the frost darkens the windows. We're bears, I say to lighten the mood. I'm seated at the cloven-foot table, I turn around it, dictating.

The routine.

It's not working.

A voice is what you'd need here.

The text by itself, it seems so sad, poor voiceless text. With all these little abandoned things. These lost stories, these little orphaned poems.

Enough to want to cry.

And then I have no inspiration.

I'm not relaxed enough.

The great champion knows how to forget, that's what they say about archers, but it holds true for everything.

Stop.

This mage business is too complicated.

So is literature.

Ugh.

And I'm the one who wanted to go on vacation. We're not going to create a new religion, lose faith, toss out the religion, and keep the music.

To have a reservoir of forms.

For some kind of gymnastics in the future.

I'm not an idiot.

It's over, I'm done.

I batten down the hatches, close the openings, seal the slits.

I'm in my cavern.

I withdraw.

Make myself over.

Total rebuild.

Cured.

I exchange my flesh for wires, rods, chips, I electronicize.

Nerve machine.

Bedtime.

I can do what I want. I'm free. I'm going back to bed. No more dictation, no more writing. You're a headache, I'm going to black, I'll trigger whatever images I want.

I don't need anybody. I'm shutting it all down, turning off the phone, heading down cellar, I want Chablis, I'll have Chablis.

I sleep at the foot of a barrel.

I ended up losing my train of thought.

The disease forced me to dive deep into my body. When there's a breakdown, you drop to all fours and dive into the skein of wires, you lose perspective, a close-up of the clock or the elbow of a pipe is a face every time. A close-up is always a face.

Oh God of pipework.

I don't remember anything but the details now, the immense and holy mess of odds and ends. But seen up close, it doesn't look like anything, I have to close my eyes to reconstruct the missing parts.

Someone's speaking to me.

Who's speaking?

If I were sick, I'd think it was a nurse.

But no, I'm radically alone.

I've got to explain the boson to you, she says.

I fall asleep tracing the coils of a labyrinth painted on the walls and ceiling.

I'm a little capsule in the dark.

It's huge to be nothing but a single point on a curve.

Think it over.

My father, at the end of his life, falling asleep in the little bed next to the canopy bed, no longer accessible, would tell me he was visiting his childhood apartment on Boulevard Malesherbes, his eyes closed, as if about to embark, gone, tiny, in the dark.

To the right.

Hallway.

Hallway.

Hallway.

To the left.

Map of the fatherboard.

Oh, vast flows of memory. I follow along, cool labyrinth, marble echo and click-click of hinged dove wings.

What a marvelous mechanism.

People used to think machines were diabolical bodies. It was like climbing a mountain to explain how a VCR worked to this same old man. Today people's feelings toward instruments are warmer, more tender.

A little more love for machines.

Now people like mathematics.

It's only in equations that they see with the naked eye.

The presence of X is deduced. Something new takes its place calmly in a calculation, like a necessary hieroglyph that was lacking.

Enter John Doe.

Phew!

Math on a human scale.

So now we can see everything on a human scale.

Home sweet home.

Particles were already there, it's enough to compel them and they exist.

Like you enter a stage.

Door opens.

New character enters.

I'm X.

He's always there only when you discover him. It's as

if you placed an inert actor in a room, he only begins to speak if you ask him a question, except he doesn't really respond to you.

He answers you to himself.

Become who you are, now I understand what was meant, it heads in both directions at once, compel something to be and it steps into the present.

A Viking ship in the middle of a river.

A horse crosses a frozen lake.

I follow the intercoiling volute, I follow it over here, no, over there.

Over here.

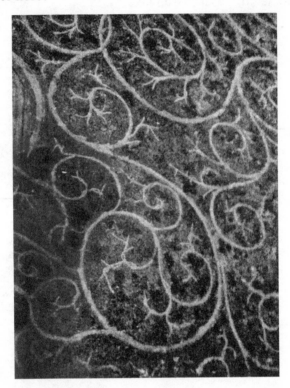

This girl in her suit looks familiar. It's crazy. Could be the girl in the photo, X in the River, if I was a novelist I'd say it was her.

Definitely.

The Viking girl taking a little dip.

I'd find something to justify this aberration.

Bosons? What are bosons? She explains a few things about particles to me.

A physicist.

Now that'd be good for a novel.

To each their own.

What if the electromagnetic force and the weak force were one and the same, she goes on with vehemence. A matter close to her heart, you can tell.

This hypothesis has been experimentally confirmed by the discovery of the bosons $W^\pm$ and Z^0 and by "exchanges" between particles.

Perfect.

By extrapolating this result, the so-called grand unified theories predict that at an energy of 1028 K, the weak and strong nuclear forces would merge into one.

A single force?

Yes, but this domain is well beyond the range of current particle accelerators, and these theories have yet to be formulated. What I can tell you is that on paper, to obtain this merging of the two forces, it takes energies on an entirely different scale than our everyday world.

There's something touching about her.

What's more, she continues, it'll be harder to find this boson than a grain of wheat lost in a lining. We won't see it. Using a huge chain of detectors, computer farms, and a prodigious computational grid, we'll measure its effects. As we have been for some time in the multi-wire chambers in particle accelerators, which resemble silk traps for invisible butterflies.

I feel like I understand her.

It's as if you suddenly opened up a house. You break down the walls and in the enlarged space, remember what delimited the rooms, as ephemeral as the light paper walls in Japan, you remember universes that were once irreconcilable.

Convalescence.

The Robinson traceability, the disease, the disease was no longer at the organs' frontier, disease pushed back, over here, I'm gone.

Air, whoosh, I drink in lungfuls.

I relax.

With the same image protocol everyone knows. To prepare for being one day in the hands of people who have to treat you with standardized methods. Imagine a beautiful sunset, they'll say right before the artificial coma. I'll turn on the music, murmurs the indifferent young nurse, something Japano-Vivaldian, have a nice vacation.

Please.

Who's the music for anyway?

A few seconds later I kill a wasp in a room with white plaster walls.

And zip! Under the microscope.
Vrrrr.

I'm not a mage at all.

It's okay.

We just have to rid ourselves of the idea.

Let's cure ourselves. We retrace, shape, purify our memories. We reach out and touch them. We get acquainted, we live with them. When you can fractionate pain, that's already good. The smallest possible non-divisible ache, an entire night spent calmly letting the grains of sand pass, one by one. Ah, to find a tiny outlet, a pin head, the tenacity of a silk thread, sssssss. And then take the morning in stages, whhhew, it'll be okay, you're completely cured, if that's what it is, it's marvelous, I holler, oh I sing, I'm the countermelody, I'm cured, I'm the second voice, above, below, basso continuo, ah, I fall, low, lower, a slur of notes, it undulates, slowly, just like that, comparisons softly coiling, the most well-known songs blended with unique feelings.

Sous le pont Mirabeau coule la Seine.

Hearing the author recite this in such a plaintive voice, everyone laughs, but it's a hit, he's right.

A real hit, one you can laugh at and love. Exactly the position you need for dancing.

Making fun of your happiness.

What a joke, what a joy.

Things come alive again, and, like a Pygmy happens to recognize a forest polyphony deep in heart of the city, an old lady listens once again to Bach chorales on the piano in the emphatic style of Marguerite Long, on the verge of tears, like a child at Midnight mass who doesn't believe, amidst the smells of pine and wax filling a mountain church.

Now I get it.

I'm in a phrase that moves.

You could say I'm new.

Awkward but airborne.

An awkward angel.

A blimp.

Today is today and that's great.

Let's celebrate.

I diffract myself.

I'm alive, yes!

I've aged visibly, now it's the opposite.

I'm in the middle of my project.

Let's dance.

Music.

Celebration alone on the edge of your bed.

Solo cure.

You know Frank Sinatra, poum-poum, he's dead, poum-poum, to be famous is so nice, poum-poum, suck my dick and kiss my ass, poum-poum, pim-pim, etc.

Extra bass.

If this goes on, I'll end up singing out loud, all by myself.

Hmm, my pillow's small like the wooden headrests in Japan, but not as hard, since its linen envelope contains an infinity of miniscule cherry pits, a ball bearing that sculpts the warm counterform of my head. Like a pharaoh on his catafalque. And there's no denying the quality of the mattress, cushy and full of feathers.

The pea is lost forever.

It works: deposition of dreams, darkness, the flesh comes undone, a moment of calm, a moment of nothing.

Oh Lord, if God were possible.

Let's pray for this liberating absence. Slowly the bandages are removed, an auto-lowering into the tomb, the body splits in two, slow motion, like a black pomegranate.

A rotting wizard, it works.

3

Everything's gray.

Everything's simple.

Luges in the fog, aviaries out of use, tennis courts in gray, afteryule, forelithe, winterfylleth, halifool. We're going to rid ourselves of stories. Surgery on the father function.

The fatherboard.

Might as well say that.

To make myself clear, I use one word to make another. Motherboard -> Fatherboard.

Just like that.

The motherboard's for connecting components, not for telling stories.

People want surgery, they want their stories removed.

In vivo.

Deliver me from evil.

But they want fresh ones, theirs-but-not-theirs, story transfusion, it's understandable.

I can relate.

Watch a war every night from your bed, without risk, a war elsewhere.

Among the Hittites.

Or the Tarahumara.

Everybody wants that.

I'm doing it. Change my story. I'm going to help others.

All I need to do is hang out my sign.

I'm an ex-mage, that'll make a good soul doctor, former

resident at Hospital X, that's what I'll put, people will come.

I'll hang a poster in one of my bedrooms converted into a waiting room.

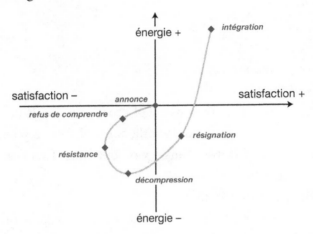

I'll tell them: It's no harder than the high jump.

Let's go!

I need an alias.

Eliphas Lévi wasn't his real name. Neither was 666. That's where you have to protect yourself.

And then, an alias is chic.

I'll take the first thing that pops into my head by putting syllables together: Zak Pierjikolm, an impossible name, at random.

It sounds good.

Engraved on a card it looks like a real person.

Opaque, different, impermeable.

Let's get the searches rolling.

Go.

Nothing.

This name does not exist.

Your search terms do not match any names.

That's the response I get.

Remove the m.

That gives us Pierjikol.

And leads to Bubble Zak.

Longchamp.

Horseracing!

I remove the l.

Zak Pierjiko.

Winner, Prix des bois noirs, Vichy.

Yipes.

Quanita Pierji, another horse name!

It's strange to choose a name that means horse three times. With Pierj, I get biblioteckacyfrowa.pl.dlibra/plain-content?id=244634.

Kaczmarski — w Czerwcu I lipcu 1934.r we... Lwowie. w ce 1u umoil\v! enla Mac. eJee ucioc %. kl. oddal RO pod opieke Matuey ora > z zaopatr.

Killer listing?

With Pier, I get: Zig zag pier, shaped like an accordion.

An image for sale, 14 cents.

Let's continue just a moment more.

Now I'm on Zak the dog in electric shocker at Whitby's East Pier, the story of a dog electrocuted by a wire.

As told in the *Whitby Gazette*.

The owner's name?

Norman Robinson (age 45).

Sic.

No more searches.

Norman? That's scary, the name of a crazy person.

In his defense, the guy said he just wanted to give someone a buzz and that Zak was electrocuted when a wire fell from the phone booth, like that.

Weird.

The Cold War?

I'm a phone booth at the end of a pier.

For a change.

Zak, you say, that already sounds a little East Coast, Cape Cod, ocean-side, so we're not far from the pier, it fits. Maybe he grew up in a big house in Brooklyn, played at his dad's big NYC hardware shop, was Salinger's classmate.

Zak.

The woman photographed in the river's name is Sharon.

It sounds good.

Zak, best friends with Sharon.

A pal to hang out with on Coney Island.

Zak.

Could also be a hot-dog vendor or a clarinetist or an ad man from the 50s, when the agencies still resembled a clothier's shop, couch geranium, imitation 18th century wood paneling, work shirts by Givenchy.

Thanks, Zak.

Cigarette holder and bright yellow opera gloves.

White magic, lite magic, better by far.

No spells cast.

No shadows behind you.

No curses.

No denunciation.

We're not going to dive into autobiography just like that.

Totally naked.

Ecce homo doesn't mean tell all.

Real names and everything.

Whoah.

People are funny.

This isn't Marathon Man.

We're in the world of today, just like everybody.

With nothing left to say.

Breathe.

You're just an organic cog.

A rod.

Don't reinvent the wheel.

I finally move.

Make it turn.

A mare turns in a meadow.

A woman turns her body into a barrier.

A man breathes the odor of flowers behind a window.

A man falls asleep with his elbows against a skull.

A man paints a dove on the glass between you and me.

He paints directly on your face.

War paint.

Let's serve some purpose, find someone.

A patient who's available.

Who's willing to play the similar enough mother.

Someone who's not on our side.

An unbiased guinea pig selected at random and not a visionary.

Not a believer.

Until now simply alive.

Weasel, mouse, viper.

My mother's a fish.

We're going to cut her in half in a barrel wrapped in chains.

And she'll come through it like a charm.

My guinea pig.

We'll say she's on the brink of death.

She's looking back.

Like everybody does at that point.

She's worried.

Feels like she's lost something.

I reassure her.

Whatever will I do with my memories? this mother asks me. They're so far away. She already has her eyes closed. I'll take care of it, no need to worry, I tell her. Let's begin.

Affective athletics.

Now there's a program for you.

It's my new sport.

Come and go in your memories, I tell her, lesson number 1, they're yours.

Oh great descent on Avallon, she says. My great (she pronounces it grrrreat) descent on Avallon, and those carafes, those carafes we drank from, great carafes, oh the great carafes of white wine, her hand traces the curve of an invisible amphora.

Go ahead.

I say softly in her ear.

Capture this scene for yourself, I think.

I send her waves.

Your memories are yours, I think intensely, you can come and go in them as you please.

Everything's alive again.

The Field of the Cloth of Gold.

We exchange our memories.

Oh I understand what you do now, she says.

My dear.

Find your stability in the skein of details that assail you, slow movement that accompanies you, slow movement of a crane, I think.

But I don't tell her.

There's no point in telling people everything.

A little girl came and told me, she continues.

But I don't know anymore.

A little girl came and told me... the house is burning. What?

Move from one memory to another, I tell her out loud.

Ahh, she says, it's magnificent. Ahh, if you knew, the brain, it's... malefic? Mephisthophelesque? What did she say? Diabolical? It's extraordinary, if you only knew, with a My Dear at the very end, whispered.

A little girl on the road told me so.

She starts over.

This mineral flesh of brain, I think, just to make an

interval for myself in the middle of this stream.

I make myself an interval between life and death.

This mineral flesh of brain.

I think.

It's miraculous, I get myself out of this stream. I find a way, in the middle, right in the middle of the grass, where it grows, I think, I hum inside myself.

I think.

She goes on. Gets annoyed, dehydrated, I... idiots... anyone who doesn't describe... beautiful landscapes?

Doesn't tell the story?

Doesn't care about beautiful landscapes?

And she continues and makes her first poem without knowing it

6 months
telegram stamp

I'll be back
my angel.

All the idiots that don't write about beautiful landscapes, she goes on, vehement, in fact by "beautiful landscapes," she meant those she could see when she closed her eyes: Oh the great descent on Avallon, oh the great, great descents, oh my dear, which we made, so fresh, grrrrreat carafes of wine, oh so sweet, a Franciscan, so beautiful, makes the descent with me, hand in hand, leather sandals, so beautiful, oh my dear... descent... so beautiful... that we made.

Fresh carafes.

Misted over, I'm the one who adds misted over.

Hmmm, fresh.

It's my turn to see what she sees.

An encampment in an abbey? I've seen stereoscopic documents where you can see a dining room that's entirely empty. High Period table and chairs, that's it.

Strangely modern and abandoned.

My abbey, empty and floating.

Then there are the times I was all alone.

I think about them.

That's the solution.

The solution for everybody.

A psalmody without regret, does that exist?

An ancient song in the modern way, is that possible?

But backwards, the ancient out in front.

Like a discovery.

If someone does that, without any preparation, if someone who's never written speaks like a book, sings like a book that speaks, speaks like a book that sings, it means everybody can, at a special time, which means there's a secret.

But I'm thinking about it.

It's like these people who suddenly burst into Aramaic or Etruscan right in the middle of a crowd.

Without ever having learned the language.

Speak in tongues.

Sing in words.

It happens.

Often on the brink of death.

But you can try it every day.

Take a country woman in the middle of the last century, still faithful to what she knows about matter and the transformation of energy. Thinking electricity is a modern form of fire, she insists on keeping the bare bulb in her kitchen turned off.

It's burning, she says.

As soon as you leave the room for a moment.

The proof: it puts out insects with a crackling hiss.

Fear of losing a precious substance.

Black night between zones of light.

Void the air from a sphere of glass.

Precious warmth, precious cold.

If you wanted to start a story, this is where you'd add

the smell of felt and steel in a black sedan. The smell of a petrol lamp, green cabbage, guinea fowl in aspic, the glint of silverware.

In short, take care to close the refrigerator as quickly as possible and even to avoid opening it for no reason, make a plan to take out the butter and milk at the same time, make a plan in advance, control the urge to get in there all the time, and so memorize what's inside, arrange your head like a cupboard, write notes on old sheets cut into labels like a captain caught in the ice flows recites the last supplies of his hold. It makes no sense anymore.

You hear just the curve of the voice, just its outline.

A far-away musical drama.

Like a horse-seller rolling out the prices in a mad litany by candlelight.

Or the same thing slowed down.

Sous le pont Mirabeau, and tatata and tatata.

Et faut-il qu'il m'en souvienne.

In a plaintive round.

Until the point of fusion is reached between irony and abandon, like the point of absolute cold or maximal heat a machine X can withstand.

Fate of snow or future sun.

If I was a musician, I'd never say anything like that, I'd use terms like timbre, pitch, intensity, I wouldn't talk about music as a long flexible tube, a black wave in the shape of an eel.

An animal.

And this method ended up extending to her entire life, in recitations of what remained to her, in songs of her treasures, as if she was rehearsing a speech for tomorrow.

Always tomorrow.

And one thing leading to another, she began to psalm her life.

Partaker in a rite for one.

Making her first and only poem.

Oh the wheat that resembled the sea.

Because I'd never seen the sea, but I saw those fields of wheat from above, where we stood with my father and, becoming a poetess for an instant, like someone who gets up in the middle of an assembly and sings in tongues, remembering the rhythm of a few long phrases learned at school, I'd never seen the sea, she continues, but the wheat fields went on and on, and the wind, she gestures to indicate trembling, waving, and the wind, and she doesn't know how to finish her sentence… it was like the sea.

That's all.

Like someone who gets up one morning and sees the gray foam of the rooftops out the window, and the folds of his or her aging skin, and starts to hum without realizing it.

I'm up early and moving.

The sun is white.

The road to the hospital, white.

Let's try.

We'll start with that.

Self-program.

Phrase my commands.

Concentrate.

It's my new sport.

We're going to put the brain together backwards, as soon as an idea comes out, like a vine, we're going to re-transplant it. Make a skein. An abandoned coil of wire, an electromagnet. We run it back, we stack, braid, join together.

Just like that.

Out comes the word we want.

And it's irresistible.

A pelican plunges into his son's bill.

Everything mixes.

It's marvelous.

One song, two voices.

Step through spaces.

It speaks.

I finally look like the little deaf boy with his hearing aid who can hear for the first time.

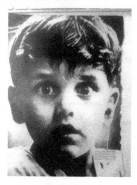

I hear all at once.

It projects forward, like a sparrowhawk, a net, gauze above water that's flowing too fast, but some of the fishes cluster into squadrons and quiver to keep still, ideas stay in place in the current.

The transitions are hard, but on the whole, it's supple.

A broken-up love song.

Does that exist?

Replace the emotive bolts with pop articulations.

Is that possible?

And this?

Modern ligaments in an ancient ballad?

Too complicated.

Forget that.

Think this over.

You remember someone for eternity because of a tiny piece of advice. Every time I make a cup of coffee, if it's instant, I think of my brother who'd say every morning in a serious tone not to use more than a spoonful, even for a big cup. If it's filter coffee, I inevitably think of her and how she insisted on filling the pan of boiling water little by little, in several steps, while filtering the coffee to save time. You always think of your grandfather when you stack up a little house of logs to make the perfect fire. Or those points of etiquette that mask an old superstition and now pass as chic, like turning over the empty shell of a soft-boiled egg and breaking it with a casual tap, The Father's Word. Avoid danger: never touch a light switch with wet hands. You could classify these bits of advice into categories by setting apart those that prevent certain death, for example, from those that make life easier, etc. But what counts is that they automatically make you think of someone, I greet a brother with every cup of instant coffee, like those crosses on the roadside in memory of X Killed Here, that you greet every day on the same curve close to home.

As if there was also some vague hope of improvement, ahh one day I'll make the coffee even better, you progress in the art of handling the pan, like a golfer works his swing for thirty years, one day you'll get it down to the milligram, the ideal dose of coffee.

These innumerable attempts are there to tell us, you'll do better the next time. Go ahead, whispers that voice to me, make a little house, add a touch of water. Voilà! say my loved ones, those at my ear, the little genie perched on my shoulder. You're making coffee, it's now, you're alive. Their voices, without any sound, vibrate in me who knows where. In my hands, in the nerve that connects my brain to my fingers. I'm alive, I'm alive. Lights flash in your memory, they replicate your movements with words. In a long phrase that's plaintive, but muscular inside.

A gray shape full of firecrackers.

Flashy articulations.

That's it!

As if you'd splashed a diplodocus skeleton with reds, blues, greens.

I dance in vibrant gray.

It's all described in the best sense.

Acrobatics in air.

I compose, de-compose myself.

Just like that.

I'll write you some beautiful landscapes.

I present a series of extremely dense layers around my palpitating heart. By leaving the point of collision for the outside, as if crossing an island end to end, you find a zone of silicon made up of 60 million detectors.

Then a transparent layer of several thousand lead tungstate crystals forming an electromagnetic calorimeter that measures the energy of charged particles. Next, a very dense layer containing a high quantity of iron that serves as a hadronic calorimeter, a particle detector sensitive to quarks, and then the solenoid itself.

There's a beautiful landscape for you.

The particles from the collision have speeds and energies so high that in order to significantly alter their trajectories and obtain information about their charge, you'd have to produce a field with an intensity of 4 teslas, 100,000 times more powerful than the earth's magnetic field.

I'm hot.

Finally, the last layer, with the highest volume, consists of the muon system, or 1,400 muon chambers distributed throughout the external parts.

I was really starting to get hot.

You could hear perch hunting at the corners of a grassbed, as electric blue kingfishers streaked after flies on the surface and an explosion of fluffy ephemerae invaded the atmosphere.

Same as irises seen behind a gate in darkness.

Nice.

Time to think about swimming.

Instead of vacillating.

Enough is enough.

I'm too hot.

I take off my black wool redingote lined with merino.

I take off my starched shirt, my celluloid cuffs.

My sock suspenders.

My woolen underwear.

I unwrap the cream-colored cotton bandage wrapped around my belly to contain my anxieties.

A mummy, maybe.

I have an enormous striped towel.
Dive.
The water level had fallen a lot.
So much at one point that the river was dry.
Right there.
For the first time, the bed is dry.

Searching behind the stakes, in a hole in the rock, we find an axe.
Viking.
There.
Right below the falls.
In a hole.
Klunk!
Hey, guys! I dropped my axe.
A Viking ship isn't going to stop just like that.

Adieu to the axe.

Let's keep moving through the landscape.

And for some time we walk on this dry bed as through a field of ruins.

Water!

The water rises further down.

That was just a dry arm of the river.

A dry moment.

The water rises.

Legs.

Belly.

Shoulders.

Feet no longer touch the ground.

And we're gone.

I let myself drift, like the unconscious logs of wood following the current.

If I could find the ideal plane of words, an unstable equilibrium on a ball that rolls in every direction.

That would be great.

Like in that game where you use a pair of wheels to both direct and stabilize a metal ball in a little wooden maze riddled with holes.

Plunk.

I float on my back.

Can I still have real experiences?

Read a manual on deer hunting.

And go deer hunting.

An experience that takes its place beside another.

I turn over.

My head in the black mirror.

I remain underwater for a long time.

Underwater.

Tendrils of bubbles rising to the surface.

The muscles crack slightly.

Cartilage crawl.

Green muscles in the shell of water.

I swim.

A character! Ten characters! I was shouting. Fiction, blood flowing again, alive again, I roar up every silty channel of my brain-heart in a motorboat. I feel like I've been frozen for a very long time.

I swim.

Breaststroke and rrrripppp, I tear myself from the terror of the liquid mass, Faaaather, Sister, Brother, I shout in time, like a galley slave with each heave of the oar, head thrown back at the tree-edged vault of sky that resembles a natural cathedral, Mooooother, like in that song that starts with an enormous bell sound, I swim while crying out to the river.

It feels good.

I've got sensation again, like the tingling in my fingers which have come back to life. Hmm, I re-occupy the electrical tracks of my neurons.

Just like that.

Let's get some more air.

Like in games that demand more and more flow, as the player progresses, armed with the maximal life points, the decor builds up in real time.

Moving forward, the story densifies.

I swim very deeply.

And return to the surface to breathe.

Breaststroke, deep breath-stroke.

Just like that.

We develop, align, compose, de-compose ourselves.

I swim.

I'm the bull swimming against the current.

The water reshapes around my arms. The grasses invent themselves and deploy.

I'm on the verge of singing all alone.

Oh little voice.

Oh Robinson, over here, the voice, the tiny voice, a speedway out of gloom. Oo-ooo Robinson, oh I've got the voice I started with, ouf, ouf, the little voice of nothing, partridges in the wheat, mice beneath the boards, ptarmigans in the stairs, eel in the grass, oo-ooo Robinson.

Robinson.

Over here.

Oo-ooo.

Over here.

There.

Right there.

Right.

A green crypt.

A suspended clearing.

She's there.

And it's so cold.

Crazy the things you think about just before you dive.

I see green grasses, raw and undulating. A bit of something, I see something... gaseous... a gaseous mass. I'm immersed in a sparkling spring... generalized liquid.

She's planted in the middle of the water.

And swimming.

She has a terrific water sense, a softness, and always so relaxed. Direct in her trajectory. A paradox in action, its cutting edge, her trainer might say. She builds up enormous speed. She carves a clean curve. Her commitment is extraordinary. She's streamlined, low, committed. In constant contact with the inside of the water.

You really know how to swim.

I've got to live this experience to the limit, she tells me, it's extraordinary to turn something complicated into ultrasimple decision, what a surprise.

I'm happy, she says.

I'm not crazy you know.

I inhabit only doable ideas that move, I'm cured of the urge to talk under a reign of terror.

I agree with you, I reply, adding, it's nice to talk.

It's my story told by me, with the inside and the outside,

that line cutting me in half is gone. What I've put myself through, she says in one breath. Half a bull under glass, no it's fine, everything's flowing, like Aladdin's lamp, the smoke, the genie, it's gone, I've rid myself of it, I'm happy, done, the thing that stops, bars the way by turning on itself, the organ on display, phhhew.

Do you understand what I'm saying?

Absolutely, I respond.

Can a mage exist without magic? I continue, a mage in a white cube.

Like an image, picture-perfect, image-perfect.

Silence.

Only you can't talk and explain at the same time. And some people think you should say some things and sing others.

To explain, say, sing and swim at once — a crowd of one.

She's not listening to me.

This is where I'm happy, she continues, as if I hadn't said anything.

And, like a child who, without knowing it, draws a scene on paper that's too big, which, I think, as in a dream, condenses several scenes, it's in these meanders that something unfolds and emerges.

I think and I tell her all this at the same time.

She looks like she understands.

This is new.

There are dimensions of space rolled up in each other, she tells me, deploying her fingers, a sheet of paper, 2, that's easy, rolled up tight, it's a line, in fact it was already a line, yet another dimension.

Try it with 4!

And how do you iron your shirts? Like this of course, in two dimensions, she imitates an iron. And here? She indicates the edge of the fabric. Do you iron here? Do you think about this dimension?

And with me?

With all my folds.

Not a few dimensions there.

And that's holding still.

If I move, it's crazy.

Right?

I swim.

An enormous, bearded mage slides into the cold water.

That's me.

Like a stick plunged into water, I get thinner.

I spiral.

I get younger.

Under the water.

Manatee.

Just like that.

I'm a fish.

I swim.

I get younger underwater.

I swim.

You cannot imagine all that a body can.

CPSIA information can be obtained
at www.ICGtesting.com
Printed in the USA
FSHW011521021219
64504FS